LAST DATE IN EL ZAPOTAL

First published by Charco Press 2024
Charco Press Ltd., Office 59, 44-46 Morningside Road, Edinburgh
EH10 4BF

A CIP catalogue record for this book is available
from the British Library.

ISBN: 9781913867843
e-book: 9781913867850

www.charcopress.com

Edited by Fionn Petch
Cover designed by Pablo Font
Typeset by Laura Jones-Rivera
Proofread by Fiona Mackintosh

2 4 6 8 10 9 7 5 3 1

Mateo García Elizondo

LAST DATE IN EL ZAPOTAL

Translated by
Robin Myers

CHARCO PRESS

1

I came to El Zapotal to die once and for all. I emptied my pockets as soon as I set foot in the town, tossing the keys to the house I left behind in the city, my credit cards, anything with my name or photograph. All I've got left are three thousand pesos, twenty grams of opium, and a quarter-ounce of heroin, which had better be enough to kill me. If not, I'll be too broke to even buy a pack of cigarettes, much less pay for a roof over my head or score some more lady, and then I'll freeze and starve to death out there instead of making slow, sweet love to my skinny bride, just as I've planned. That should get me through for sure. But I've missed the mark before and I always wake up again. I must have some unfinished business to take care of.

I've been wanting to take this trip for ages. It's my last wish in a life stripped of all other ambitions or desires. I've been letting go of everything that once tethered me to this earth. My wife died and then my dog died, too. I burned bridges with family and friends, sold the TV, the dishes, the furniture. It was like a race against myself to see if I could scrape up enough smack and enough dough to clear the hell out before I ended up completely paralyzed. I needed to lose everything first – it was something I had to do. Where I'm going, I won't even need my body any more. But this sack of bones has been following me the whole way, and I had no choice but to drag it along with me.

Other than that, all I've brought is the can with the kit. That's where I keep my pipe, my spoon, my syringes, the whole toolbox. That's where I store the cash, too. I bought this notebook in the bus station, because I know there won't be much in the way of entertainment before I die, and I don't want to go crazy. I think I need to spell it all out. Not for anyone else, though. Just for myself, so I can understand what's been happening to me this whole time. I need to describe what dying feels like, because no one sticks around to tell the tale. Except for me. I'm still here, and I'm getting closer. I know what it feels like to live in limbo, to start slipping over to the other side. I'm a kind of living corpse now. That's how people see me. I can't just blurt it out to anyone, not out loud, because the living can no longer hear what I have to say. I hope no one reads this, just to avoid any misunderstandings. I hope they don't even find it. Better if they burn it or throw it in the trash or dump it in the grave along with whatever's left of me.

I've come all the way out here because when I die I don't want anyone to wake me up again. I don't want anyone to find me and haul me out of bed or dress me up or put the colour back into my face. I don't want the rigmarole: the rites, the tears, the pretty words. I want people to say I renounced everything, like a saint. That I abandoned all earthly ties and matters of the flesh and travelled alone into the jungle to face my death head-on. I want them to think of me and say 'How brave' and 'Not just anyone can pull that off'. People think you do this sort of thing out of cowardice, but no. It's just what happens when you realise what we're all bound for, where we're all going. Everything becomes meaningless, except for this. This does make sense. At least to me. This is all I want to figure out.

I'd never heard of El Zapotal and I don't really know why I came here. All I wanted was to reach the end of the line, the ends of the earth. But this isn't what I'd imagined. Here, the human world peters out, and then there's just jungle and hills. It's said that people get lost in the bush, outside of town, and they lose their minds; that they see monsters and catch a fever that makes them bleed from their pores. All day long, you can hear the cicada-drone muddling with the blare of the chainsaws that the village men use to cut down trees in a frantic struggle against nature, fighting to invade its territory. Every felled tree is a triumph that leaves a wake of sterile vacant lots behind, enveloped in a hot, foul, stifling fog, desolate plots that can no longer be used for anything at all, ravaged of any remaining life. Meanwhile, the weeds rise faster than they can be cut, and they overrun the town, devouring streets and houses as they grow. During the day, the men grapple with these weeds in the oppressive heat, and at night, trying to distract themselves and forget, they drink and fight until they pass out.

From what I've heard, the village was founded as an encampment for the lumber trade, because that's all this place has to offer, the only thing of interest. To encourage the expansion of the settlement, the government brought in prostitutes from all over the state, and the outpost started by lumberjacks and whores became El Zapotal. Besides the mostly humble houses, there's a scattering of farms, a couple of sawmills, a chapel, two abandoned haciendas, a convenience store, and a cantina. The dirt road into town exists only for the lumber lorries, laden with amputated trunks, plus the occasional bus, like the one that brought me here. These are the only means of transport into this wasteland, supplying enough beer, cigarettes and Coca-Cola to give the village an illusory air of civilisation.

Near the bus station, I found a guesthouse, or the closest thing to it. The landlord, Don Tomás, rented me a room on the second floor of an unfinished concrete structure with a tin roof. It overlooks the street on one side, and the backyard with the Don's water tank on the other. I pay a hundred pesos a night for this pigsty. There's nothing but a cot, a table, a dresser, and a shoddy, doorless latrine out back with a seatless toilet and a little sink. The cement walls are already cracked and a reddish light filters through the flowered curtains in the afternoons. It's a perfect room to die in.

The Don asked what brought me to El Zapotal, and since I didn't expect him to understand, I told him I was on holiday. He said not to smoke in the room because people like me always burn the mattresses, he'd had a bunch of fires already. I told him not to worry and gave him six hundred pesos to buy myself a few days' peace. Then I stretched out in bed to smoke some opium. I'd just arrived, after all, and there was no need to rush.

I remember that I started getting drowsy, and I felt as if I had a mouthful of cotton moulding itself to my teeth. Little by little, my nostrils went numb, my eyeballs, my earlobes. I was engulfed in a pleasurable feeling that travelled my entire body, from my toes to the tips of my hair.

That's how it begins.

2

Smoking opium clears the fog in your head. Your thoughts take on the presence and materiality of physical objects, like you could touch them. People say it makes you sleepy, but I never feel as awake as when I smoke. Under the soft plumes of vapour, your visions hidden in the basements of the mind, impossible to capture when you're really conscious, they unfurl in harmonious permutations, appearing and fusing together with the clarity of an open vista. You even feel good. You feel smart and refined, and strong in your limbs, and if anyone knocked on your door you'd welcome them in with tea and cookies. When I smoke opium, it's like I'm lying in a room filled with works of art, marble tables, velvet armchairs. A castle, a millionaire's mansion. I feel like I'm the millionaire, and that this exuberant, voluptuous kingdom is mine, all mine.

You start drifting off and your dreams creep in like a bass line, a song in the background that you stop hearing after a while, even though it's still there. The first thing I see whenever I begin to fade out are flocks of birds in the sky, winging in unison, not touching each other, like a cloak that flutters and palpitates in the wind. I know it's a distant memory, something I saw from a car when I was little, as my dad drove along a highway, crossing an infinite plain of monotonous golden grasses. I can't come up with any other context for it; I don't know where we were going or where we'd been, but from the back seat I looked out at that huge, ominous presence with a mix of fright and fascination.

Confronted with this singular living entity that contracts and expands in the sky, I always feel like I can see a presence, sometimes more human, sometimes almost animal, as if the sky itself were a parted veil, offering a glimpse of a face that peers out and watches me, looks after me. It greets me for a moment, then vanishes again. It's a familiar presence, but I struggle to recognise it, and just as it starts to make sense to me, the cloud of birds contracts again. The presence hides itself away and won't come back if I wait. It only returns when I forget, letting it catch me by surprise once more.

This vision soothes me, lulls me. I fight against the exhaustion that wells up overwhelmingly as soon as the image flashes into my mind. I stay awake just so I can keep watching, and when I can't nod off, I picture it and always plummet right into sleep, like a corpse. In that haphazard movement, I see panoramas sharpening into focus before they disappear again, and I look for some thread I can follow through their hatches, passageways, and dark alleys, into chambers connected by vaults and stairs. I make my way among their vertices and edges, through their undersoil and the hollows beyond their walls, losing myself in the texture of each vision until, as in all dreams, I forget I'm dreaming and let myself be swept along by these improbable storylines that lead into the farthest reaches of that world, both intimate and foreign to me.

In one, I suddenly found myself walking through a lush garden filled with marble statues like Greek gods, but bony ones, covered in wounds and bruises, and when I got closer I realised that I knew them. They were my friends from the trap house. I hadn't seen some of them for ages. Mike was there, and he'd been dead for a long time, although maybe he wasn't entirely dead after all. He was very still, but his lips were moving. 'Are you seriously joining us already, man? Come on, get out of here, this is no place for you…'

I understood from his words that they'd all ended up here, that El Zapotal was one giant trap house, and that instead of escaping I'd just found my way back to the start. Mike told me to go back to the city, that this was an exclusive club – which was odd, because he was never like that, he'd always welcome you in and share whatever he had on hand.

'What bug crawled up your ass, dude?' is all I said. 'Since when have you been such a snob? You got the shakes or what?'

Drifting through dreams, I felt a dog licking my hand, as if trying to wake me, and I opened my eyes and looked around the room. There was a very skinny old woman bustling about. She acted like my mother, but she couldn't have been, because my mother died giving birth to me. Maybe she'd ended up here, too. She looked worried, and for a while I thought she must also want me to leave, retreat to the city. Then I realised she was unsettled by the mess. 'What mess, lady?' I said. 'There's nothing here.' And she pointed at the colourful junk lying all over the place, dishes and tinted glass vases and statues of exotic animals I figured Mike must have packed in a secret suitcase after stealing them from some household or other, hoping to squirrel them away. They were fragile, beautiful, maybe priceless objects, and they shattered one by one as I tried to straighten them up. Why wasn't there a kitchen in the room, the woman said, how was I ever going to eat anything. She made me promise to buy myself an electric stove so that I could at least make my own coffee.

I tried to ignore Mike and the lady so that they'd leave me alone. I'd left the city just two days before; I couldn't believe they'd already tracked me down. It was like they'd come just to breathe down my neck, rattle around the room, and rearrange my stuff, purposely keeping my nerves on edge, refusing to let me rest. It made me nervous, how they hurried around like circus dwarves, rummaging in drawers and searching hidden corners of the room. I feared they'd steal my kit, ruin my plan. Mike removed the loose brick in the wall that exposed the underground tunnels, which had to be a good thing, I remember thinking; a good place to seek shelter if I felt lonely or tired, if it all became too much.

I don't know what happened with Mike. Maybe he said he'd wait for me down there, underground. I remember the lady sat down beside me on the mattress and stroked my head for a long time. I felt her thin, bony hands and wondered if the Pale One had come for me, if her lullaby would send me into slumber, never to return.

3

When I opened my eyes that morning, I realised I was still alive, it had all been one of those dreams you have when you smoke opium, I'd fallen for it again. So I made a date with the lady. I'd never been much for breakfast and didn't intend to start now, but as I started to cook my fix I saw that the lighter was spent and I wouldn't even be able to smoke a cigarette, so I was forced to walk to the store for another one.

The streets were deserted. There were more dogs than people, and some barked until they realised I was one of them, gaunt and homeless. Then they followed me peacefully. Maybe they were hoping I'd drop dead and become the day's meal. Still, I felt a kindness in their presence, as if they knew I needed company and guidance as I went.

The few people I passed – farmers and drunks, a few women wrapped in shawls – all glanced at me sidelong and pressed on, as if I wasn't there, as if they didn't want to know I was there. Pale and ragged, a group of four or five teenagers studied me from the bushes partway along the route, whispering among themselves. I paused from time to time and tried to figure out where they were hiding, but I couldn't spot them. When I carried on, I heard them again, glimpsed them from the corner of my eye as they followed me through the trees and ivy. They even managed to lob a rock at me, hitting my shoulder, before they darted off behind the broken boards of what looked like an abandoned house. A few metres on, I spied another group of kids playing in the dirt, but they screamed and scattered when they saw me heading their way. They left all their bottle caps on the ground. I still don't know if they were mocking me or truly afraid; either would have made sense.

The sun is fierce in this place, and the heat and the sweat make my mouth dry and my body itch even worse than usual. Mosquitos never bite me – my blood probably tastes awful – but even so, I feel a constant prickly irritation that makes me want to yank my skin off. I can't wait to get out of it.

In the distance, you can make out the cracked pink walls of the enormous haciendas gone to ruin, consumed by weeds. They look like they're from another time, vestiges of some settlement before El Zapotal. They could be mayoral buildings or historic monuments if they hadn't been doomed to abandonment, the village deliberately cut off from them. I'm convinced that something must have happened there, a long time ago, for those fincas to be left to the mercy of the jungle. You can still feel it. They have the grim, ominous air of places frozen in time, both absent and present, like I am. I bet they'd be a good place for me: I could go and find a spot to sit and lean back among the wreckage and build my kingdom there. I'd like to see them from up close, but the entrance seems impenetrably overgrown.

I wanted to buy a normal candle at the store, but they only had votive candles. The old clerk kept shooting glances at me, with that mix of suspicion and disgust

I'm used to by now. It doesn't startle or bother me any more. In fact, it's kind of fun to disgust people, to see them shudder in horror, as if I were an insect. I behaved, though, because if I get barred from buying stuff in the only store in town, my adventure will be over even sooner than planned. Besides, no one scorns money. It's a palpable thing, something that belongs to this world.

I bought a votive candle with the image of Saint Jude on it, plus a lighter, cigarettes, and water. Also some plain yogurt. It might not last long in this weather, especially since I don't have a fridge, but my gut isn't what it used to be. In my extensive experience, there are only a few things I can always digest, and yogurt is one of them. Some people can digest anything but yogurt, but for me it's sometimes all I can keep down. I drink it straight from the container and fill my belly, not because I'm hungry, but because otherwise I'll be too weak to get out of bed and cook up another fix.

As I left the store, a big, burly guy approached me, a real macho type: hat, moustache, cowboy boots, the whole nine yards. He wore an eye-catching necklace strung with an ornate cross and images of the Virgin, the Trinity, and several saints. He planted himself right in my path, looked me up and down, and introduced himself after a stomach-turning pause.

'Afternoon,' he said. 'Rutilo Villegas, at your service.'

He put on a show of friendliness without holding out his hand: how was I doing, was I visiting from out of town. Classic cop stuff. Although he clearly wasn't an actual police officer – there's no money even for that around here – but some evangelist who cherry-picks his charity cases, which makes him think he has the right to meddle in other people's business just because he can. I sensed I had to be careful with this guy. I wouldn't want him snooping around my room, that's for sure.

'Afternoon, sir. Yeah, I'm just passing through. Already on my way out, actually,' I told him, smiling broadly as I backed off. He followed at a careful distance.

'Well,' he said, 'we've certainly seen our fair share of degenerates like yourself. Folks who only come here to stir up trouble. Don't think for a minute we'll just sit back and watch as you go around disrespecting young ladies and stealing from honourable citizens.'

It didn't seem worth explaining that the pleasures of the flesh were long behind me, that the local young ladies were about as enticing to me as a T-bone steak: my stomach heaved at the very thought of how hard it would be to chew and digest one, no matter how juicy and delicious.

'Take it easy,' I insisted, 'I'm passing through, that's all.'

He stared as if he didn't believe a word. 'You have no idea,' he said. 'No one just passes through this place. They always stay put in the end. And there are already too many of us.'

I glanced around. It was practically a ghost town.

'I'll be long gone by the time anyone complains about me, boss. I'm not like the others, you'll see.'

That's what I said, as confidently as I could manage, and so he wouldn't think I'd come to steal, I clapped him on the back, offered to buy him a beer and gave him a hundred pesos. After all, it was true: I didn't have much time left and it would be a shame to leave my money unspent.

He just stood there looking at me. People do that: they stare as if you were a viscous, strange-smelling alien, fix you with a combination of terror and resentment. As if your very presence were tantamount to taking a dump in their living room. It's chilling, this hostility, because at the end of the day these people don't even know me, don't know who I am. It's like being a foreigner – not just from another region or country, but from beyond the human race altogether. Which I am. I'm not from this world. Like I said, I'm just passing through. It takes people a while to grasp. When it finally hits them, when they get that you're in a totally different gear, they don't know whether to feel sorry for you or punch you in the face. They simply can't wrap their heads around it.

Relaxing a little, the guy took pity on me. Go see the priest, he suggested. Go to AA. I said I didn't see the point, I never went to confession. And you could meet drunks just about anywhere, they were strewn all over town.

'Don't be sarcastic,' he said. 'That's what's got you into this mess.'

Then he launched into an evangelical tirade, warning me that I'd better accept the light of God, take my fate by the reins.

'No matter how hard it is,' he said. 'Sure, it's a long and winding road. But you have to come to your senses. You'll need all your willpower to take the right path. Listen to what I'm telling you.'

He was probably right. I wanted to wind things down because the itch was coming on – the other itch, the kind that starts with butterflies in your stomach but soon intensifies into cramps and stabbing pains. And since I didn't want to end up drenched in cold sweat and hearing voices, I may have been a little more abrupt than necessary when I cut him off, told him to mind his own business and let me die in peace. Rutilo just clicked his tongue and shook his head, and as I walked off I heard the asshole say: 'Don't go expecting us to give you a proper burial in this town, young man.'

And I only thought: fine with me, dude. No skin off my back.

4

Sometimes I wonder why I don't just shoot up a big fat dose and get it over with. Then I remember that dying is no easy feat. Inevitable, sure, but not always easy. That's part of why I came here. In the city, you can't even give up the ghost in peace. I tried a few times, but they always brought me back, and I'm still here, never managed to take the leap. Like I said, I must have some unfinished business to take care of. Dying, though – it's one of the most beautiful things there is. It's not scary or confusing like people say. I think they talk like that because the idea of eternal rest is too tempting. Because if they didn't, then everyone would want to die.

No, there's nothing scary about death. It's just like slipping all the way into some warm, narrow space, like a big vagina, then slipping out again onto the other side. You feel light, free, as if your body were a weight you'd been carrying around your whole life and finally shed, or as if life were a drill boring into your kidney and someone pulled it out at last. *I'm home,* you feel, *I'm staying here forever.* It's like the world finally gives you enough room to see your own thoughts, and the vision is like the night sky, full of stars. You just stand there and watch them get snuffed out one by one, the whole expanse going dark and empty. It's incredible. Such a sense of peace.

And then they start to revive you. What a bunch of tactless fucks, frankly. Imagine you're asleep and you hear a knock at the door, slowly at first, then louder and faster and more insistent, until you have no choice but to get up and yell at them to fuck off. That's when you jolt awake. And one thing's for sure: it's not confusing to leave for the other side. What's confusing is when you wake up covered in vomit, surrounded by people freaking out, paramedics slapping you around and hollering about how you were about to die. Sometimes even the cops are there. You feel a cramp in your chest when they jump-start your heart, and your lungs burn when you draw air back in, as if it were the first time you'd ever used them. Your whole body tingles, because all the blood that had flowed into your brain and innards starts seeping out into your limbs, and that's when the shakes and the vertigo start. I figure it's more or less what being born must feel like. And I'd much rather die, to be honest. When I get resuscitated, I always come back pissed off, fed up, head pounding, because the Naxolone doesn't just revive you, it also sends you straight into withdrawal. All you want is to die all over again.

Of course, if you saw someone else go over the edge, you'd resuscitate them too. Or at least you'd try. Jairo didn't come back and neither did Mike. But it seemed right, the way they went. You could tell it worked out for them, they found what they'd been searching for. They looked just like a junkie when he hits the sweet spot: gentle, relaxed, eyes rolled skyward, like saints in an old painting. As for my Valerie, that's another story: she just OD'd, plain and simple, and there was nothing else to be done. But we always tried. It was like a courtesy we shared. Even though no one thanked you when it worked. On the contrary: 'You should've let me croak, asshole.' That's what they say when you bring them back. Which is understandable, or at least I understand it. When you've run into death as often as I have, life takes on another meaning. The place I'm talking about isn't meant for the living, and when you've gone away and come back as many times as I have, you don't really belong to this world any more, either.

I'd say you start existing in a kind of limbo. That's where I live now, that's what this whole town is: limbo. That's what heroin is, too. You're halfway between the world of the living and the world of the dead, and neither wants to deal with you. That's the price to pay for your return trip to the other side. But any price is worth the peace you find there. I think that's what makes an addict: not the drugs, but that sense of peace. You'd give anything to feel it again. You understand that we come into this life to leave it, to find that place, so that's what you keep looking for. You have no choice.

That's the hard part. If you get it right, the line between the rush and your own death is so thin that you get there right when you least expect it. There's no pain, no time: just peace, lots of peace. It's a tricky dose, and you spend the end of your life groping around for it. Some go too far, and you can see in their eyes that they grappled with the anguish, choked on it. As if they'd drowned in the ocean. But they actually drowned inside themselves, in their own vomit. That's how it was for my Valerie. I don't think there's anything worse than that. That's the risk we all run. That's why you can't go around doing whatever you want, can't take it lightly. You have to think things through. Lots of junkies plan trips like this one and never arrive because they simply don't live long enough. But I've been playing this game for ages and I'm still here. I'm in the big leagues now.

5

I spent a long time, maybe days, lying on the cot and staring at a corner of the dresser. The wood seemed to change texture, as if rippling with a tremulous wave, like a film of water, a fibrous, living flesh that breathed and writhed. The angles of the dresser formed massive cliffs, vast walls of a filiform rock, solid matter that had taken centuries to trickle down over itself. It was like having a vista onto the end of the world. Astonishing, but also simple in a way that brought me a profound sense of fulfilment and calm. It didn't raise questions or concerns. It was a spectacle that will carry on until the universe itself disintegrates. I could have watched until I passed out and away, utterly serene, as my body gathered dust and withered into a mummy and bloomed with fungi and wildflowers.

I don't know how or when it happened, but I found myself wandering the streets of the village at night. I don't think getting out of bed was a conscious choice. It's been months since I've had any willpower at all, and I'm generally incapable of decisions beyond the ones my body takes to sustain itself. I think it had something to do with knowing I'd have to spend another night in this world. That's what must have propelled me up and out: the visceral urge to feel and find life and warmth, even where there isn't any. Or maybe my body was just thirsty, or hungry. I'm not sure. The lady makes me forget things sometimes.

So I went, even though I didn't expect to find anything out there. My body weighed me down, lurching and dragging its feet along the dusty dirt roads, plunged into hermetic darkness. The village always shuts off and goes to sleep as soon as the sun sets, and it takes on a phantasmagorical mood. The damp, warm air smells like a mix of wet earth, gutter water, wood smoke, and cow manure. I could hear men's voices and banda music in the distance. All I could make out were the silhouettes of a few concrete houses in the brush, black patches against a starry sky.

There's no public lighting in this town except by the cantinas. People flock to these fleapits for the same reason as moths flit around lamps at night: they're the only reference point, the only place to orient yourself in the physical space of the village. That night, a wake of slouched drunks unfurled through the streets, their faces slick with vomit, snot, tears, drool, and dirt, a path that led to the tavern, and the music got louder and more enveloping with every step. Two blocks away, you could follow the smell of rancid beer without even needing the glow of a halogen bulb, placed there to guide the steps of would-be patrons like a lighthouse flashing across the open sea. A Corona Light sign hung over the front door, partly illuminated by the bulb that also revealed the name of the bar: El Rincón de Juan.

Outside, a kid of around eighteen was beating the shit out of a fifty-something guy. Other men shouted and placed their bets. Hordes of stray dogs circled them all, looting scraps from the garbage bags that someone had left out by the kitchen door. The older man bled from the mouth and nose, yelling and staggering, while the boy hadn't even broken a sweat. He was using the older man as a punching bag. Between swipes, he dragged on a cigarette and chugged a beer he'd set down by a bush. Someone was going to have to break up the fight, but nobody did: they all laughed and jeered, and between the blows crunching into the man's face and his blood-burbling breath, I overheard two drunks discussing the virginity of his daughter.

I stepped inside the cantina, into the raucous music and the engulfing reek of beer and piss. The white-tiled walls gave it look of an abandoned slaughterhouse, or a half-refurbished public toilet. There was nothing but a bar and a few plastic tables and chairs. In the back, men lined up to use the john, a concrete cube stuck to the wall and separated from the rest of the space by a shower curtain. In a far corner, another group of men stood in a circle and passed bills around, but I couldn't see what they were betting on. Maybe dice.

The lighting was too fierce for a brothel, which is what the place appeared to be. Several corpulent women swayed on a makeshift dance floor among the tables, and others sat in their clients' laps, many too tanked to speak without drooling onto their chins, their shirts drenched with sweat, the whores' necklines low and brimming. Some men danced alone, trying to feel up the girls, who snubbed them, and so they danced with other men instead, grinding shamelessly as onlookers cackled. Good old Rutilo was there, the town cop, but my presence didn't seem to interest him now that he was spending my hundred pesos on girls and beer. Everyone's eyes were red and glassy, their foreheads gleaming with sweat. I reckoned there must be meth in town. People shouted and shoved and scuffled, and they were hyped, holding their liquor far too well, or not at all; they doubled over, stumbled, could barely stay upright, and even so they kept drinking, as if their thirst could never be quenched.

I haven't got drunk for years. Long before the alcohol takes effect, my muscles start to ache and I get dizzy and shaky, like a bad case of the smack jitters. But my mouth and body felt dry, and I was sure that asking for a glass of water in a place like this would be a recipe for dysentery, so I ordered a beer at the bar and sat down in a plastic chair to drink it. I wanted to enjoy the presence of other living beings, watch them unnoticed for a while. It seemed like lots of outsiders have ended up here too, at the end of the line: alcoholics, army deserters, fugitive criminals, all working in the sawmills or cutting lumber in the jungle. They share the same jobs and sometimes the same roofs; they share women and children; they have the same friends, bottles, cigarettes, and venereal diseases, no doubt about it. They spend all day outdoors and then trudge back inside to piss away their salaries, to forget themselves. Here, everyone was like me: the living dead, dragging their feet through town, their eyes unfocused. I'd give anything to get drunk, to savour oblivion again. In my terminal state, so to speak, I'm numb to all feeling, immune to inebriation, and there's only one thing I desire or enjoy.

That's what I tried to explain to the girl who came and sat down beside me. She had dark skin, a broad nose, full lips, and dark glossy hair all the way down to her waist. She wasn't as chubby as the others, but only because she was still young: she couldn't have been any older than seventeen. She pressed her hip against mine and asked me to buy her a beer. Maybe she thought I smelled like money. This could be my last drink with a woman, so I bought her one. She tried to talk over the music, but I couldn't hear her. Her voice drowned in the background noise and reached me muffled, as if from very far away. Drunk men yelled at her as they passed, nagging her to dance, but she stayed to finish her drink.

During a pause in the music, she asked where I was from. From the city, I told her. Then she asked where I was going, and I told her that too. I said I was heading straight for the land of the dead, and it was like she didn't really understand, or at least she didn't seem surprised. She just looked me up and down and said, 'Are you one of those guys who worship the Señora?'

I found her question odd.

'What señora?' I asked.

'The Lady,' she answered. 'Death. There are a bunch of people like that around here.'

She took a sip of beer and smiled, smoking a cigarette she must have extracted from my pack without me noticing.

'No, nothing like that,' I said. 'I don't worship anyone.'

She placed a hand on my knee.

'Because she shows up every night around here,' she said. 'Or almost every night. They say she's the owner. She comes in to check up on things, and then someone gets stabbed, or falls drunk off the cliff, or their heart bursts from smoking meth. You might see her if you stick around.'

I felt her stroking my leg, but I was past reacting. I turned toward the group of men standing and crouched in a semi-circle, shouting and tossing money around, and I realised they were betting on bug fights. I'd learn later that the men collect them in the jungle and bring them back in matchboxes to make a buck or two at night. They were watching two yellow scorpions locked in an embrace, frenetically trying to sting each other.

She smiled and insisted: her hand slipped up to my crotch and grabbed my dick, her eyes fixed on mine.

'Don't you want to meet her? Come on,' she said, smiling still, 'all you have to do is rent a room.'

I wondered if she was serious. I just looked at her for a moment. I looked at her large, damp eyes, sunk deep into her skull, her keen white teeth, exposed to me – and then something started happening to her, and it was just like what happened to the dresser in my bedroom. Her skin went translucent, as if I could see straight through it. I watched her blood streaming through every capillary, the protruding angles of her bones set into her flesh, her soft, warm entrails pulsing in her belly. And I saw her flinch, recoil. She turned towards a friend sitting nearby, a thin, effeminate man with a moustache edging the corners of his mouth. For the first time, I noticed the presence of three men around us, eavesdropping on our conversation.

'This one's a fag,' she said, and turned to go. But another of the men, small and solid, took her by the arm and held her there.

The tall, feminine man came over to me. 'Is that so?' he said. 'Because there's something for everybody here, hon.'

He took my hand, caressed it. I didn't pull away, not even reflexively. Everything seemed so far away. Behind him, I heard the voices of the other two men talking to him, talking about me: 'Ask him who he is, ask him what he wants… tell him we'll get him whatever he's looking for, but there's no such thing as a free lunch.'

I lifted my eyes to look at him directly. Besides the slender man and the sturdy short one gripping the girl by the arm, there was another. It was the kid who was beating up the older guy a little while ago. His face was intact, but his knuckles were stamped with fresh red wounds, his t-shirt stained with blood, and he still looked charged up after the fight. All three pinned me with their glassy stares, and they made me nervous – what were they doing here? Either people were just really friendly in this joint, or it was all a scam to lure me into some dark alley, kick the shit out of me, and rob me blind. It all felt increasingly like when a group of children discover some strange insect and flip it over for a better look. They'd start yanking the wings off soon.

The whole thing worried me because I had the can with the kit in my pants pocket, right by my balls. I wasn't about to leave it in a room where anyone could steal it. No matter how captive I was to my own delirium, the kit's the one thing I'd bring with me to the gates of the underworld. If I were to lose it, I'd have to throw myself off a cliff or something.

I sized things up. That container of yogurt was probably the only thing I'd eaten in forty-eight hours, give or take. I wouldn't stand a chance in a fight, and if I tried to run I wouldn't make it to the door, let alone the corner. I saw how wrecked they were, their lizard eyes so dilated they'd gone completely black, steady, cold, and then I got it. They were in that phase of drunkenness when you chance onto something and can't decide if you want to punch it, nurse it, fuck it, eat it, or run for your life. Even they couldn't fully understand what was happening to them. Sober, most people avoid me altogether. Drunk, everything's more complicated.

I couldn't explain it. I'd already tried: you become an exotic bug, a jot of faecal matter from another dimension, and you spark a kind of fascination in people, somehow both frivolous and morbid. Most just cross the street as soon as they see you coming; they watch you sidelong, revolted. They think you're dirty, and it's true that your body is pumped with poison, rotting, even though you're still alive. But they don't understand that your soul is actually light, and brilliant, and that's what really scares them: you're not bound to the same mundane hopes and worries that govern everyone else. All our desires and anxieties have been reduced to the quest for stillness, for bliss, for peace. For the lady. We've sacrificed everything for it, like monks. Or saints, more like it − just passing through, no longer of this world. When people drink and do drugs, when they lose their inhibitions, they also lose their fear, and then they're not afraid to approach you any more. They come up to us because they know where we're going, and they bring all kinds of tasks and messages they want us to convey to the other side.

In the cantina, things slowly descended into delirium. We talked, or we yelled − or they yelled − for a long time. I think I bought a round of drinks, and we ended up sitting together at a plastic table, where they made me eat a bowl of chicken soup I couldn't finish. I found myself between Rubí, the seventeen-year-old prostitute who kept fondling my knees and telling me how skinny I am, and Chachi, the short, stocky guy, who turned out to be a Central American migrant who'd got stuck halfway to the States when he took a wrong turn that landed him in El Zapotal. Now his dead end is his home.

Dozens of bottles vanished before my eyes. My companions drank them like water, faster than I'd ever seen anyone drink water, as we listen to Uriel, the dreamy homo sprawled across the table, borderline comatose, talking about how what really gnaws away at his insides, what poisons his soul, what's killing him at a slow simmer, is the loneliness seething in this place, infecting everything. You can feel it everywhere you go, which actually makes it a lot like death: no one escapes its grip.

Listening to the younger ones, like Rubí and the other guy − Beto by name, the kid from the fight − I understood that the only thing they wanted, their sole, all-consuming ambition, was to get out of town. In response to the others' nostalgic sermonising, Rubí only nodded, staring absently into space, and Beto shouted and thrashed, as if itching to tear the place apart, but he never knocked over so much as a single glass.

'I don't care about any of that stuff,' he said, 'because I know I'll make it out someday. There's nothing for me here. I'm clearing off…'

'But what about Chela?' Rubí said.

'What chela?' he asked, his eyes darting around the empty bottles of chela – beer – with a mixture of confusion and rage, because he knew, deep down, what she was talking about.

'Chela, you moron. Arcelia, the daughter of the dude whose face you just destroyed. Didn't you fuck her and get her pregnant?'

'So?' he said. 'If the kid is really his father's son, then he's getting out of here too.'

'So what?' she yelled. 'What does it matter?'

'It's the only thing that matters,' he replied.

It was a shame, because this boy was already all the man he'd ever be, and if he were actually capable of leaving he would have done it a long time ago. His son would probably never leave, either. None of us was going anywhere. It's a reality everyone seems to know and accept with a sense of resignation, but it was moving to see someone still losing sleep over it.

I couldn't even finish the first beer I ordered. I watched the others pass into a kind of alcoholic furore, but I was having a different experience altogether. Opium and the dope make it hard to think, but it's even harder for me to feel. Things parade before me in the distance, and the only reminder that I'm alive is the itch and the stomach ache I get before the rush is over and I need more. If I stay high, which is what I aspire to most of the time, I don't even feel that.

When your mind is no longer preoccupied with sensation, with seeking pleasure and dodging pain and disgust, there's a void that opens up, and it starts to fill with shadows, fantastical forms sculpted from the residues of sanity that wash up on the shores of consciousness. Your memory falters, and you fall into a spiral of oblivion that corrodes everything your life once was. But some still-active part of the brain recycles everything that's been buried and anaesthetised, turns it all into a kind of perpetual daydream, totally indistinguishable from everyday life. Reality takes on the bizarre texture of hallucination, and your memories of your life and your dreams become more or less indistinguishable: vague, fragmentary, garbled, and absurd.

Inside the bar, the light never changed, and the place never emptied out. It was impossible to track the passing of time. There was a dingy back room I hadn't noticed at first, with only a cot and a chair inside, and the women kept filing in and out with their clients. I was just waiting to see if the owner showed up, that lady everyone went on about. I asked my friends if Death really did run the place. Everyone said yes.

'Then why is it called El Rincón de Juan?' I asked.

'Juan is the Lady's assistant,' Rubí answered.

'Some say he's her lover,' Chachi added.

'More like her manwhore,' Beto blurted, a mischievous glint in his eye.

Rubí cut them off. 'Either way, she's the boss.'

Slumped over the table, Uriel shifted his glittery eyes towards me and smiled. 'They say Juan's the Devil.'

He said it with a look of utter seriousness.

'The Devil's name is Juan?' I repeated, and I laughed too. 'Look, if the Lady is Death and Juan's the Devil, then there must be a God around here somewhere, right?'

Beto looked baffled. 'Of course there's a God,' he said.

'But he never sets foot in this town.'

'Juan's not the Devil,' Chachi said, 'he's just the bouncer. But he doesn't always let you in.'

'That's why there are so many stranded souls waiting at the gates,' Uriel slurred from his stupor, still flopped over himself, surrounded by towers of empty glasses.

They explained: the Lady is the top dog, the boss of the whole place, though no one's ever actually seen her. Beto said she built the haciendas in the jungle, that she was a rich broad who lost her mind: they served as her fincas first, but then she turned them into cloisters, then jails, then military barracks. That at one point they'd been occupied by French settlers, army deserters, and subjected to a long siege, that all kinds of atrocities were committed inside. That they'd been abandoned because the sanitary conditions were horrific, because the unburied bodies had piled up and started swarming with disease, and the haciendas had deteriorated over time.

Beto said he knew these things better than anyone because he was born in El Zapotal, not like all the others who'd turned up since, and he spoke in the present tense of a distant era, as if time didn't pass in the village at all. He said it was possible to reach the haciendas, he knew people who could take you there, through the jungle, and they're full of old junk and piles of still-dressed bones, he said the town and the jungle are plagued with the souls of all those people, and other people too, lost souls, and sometimes you can see them wandering through the trees, stuff like that.

Uriel and Rubí pulled out a meth pipe and I unwisely took a hit. At first it picked me up, but then I felt a jolt of anxiety so intense that all I wanted was some lady to shake it off. I retreated to the bathroom several times to try and snort a little at least, but there wasn't much privacy behind the shower curtain. Chachi was onto me as soon as I started itching for real. He brought a scorpion to the table and kept urging me to smoke the stinger. People told him to stop being such a disgusting sadist and I ignored him, but then he cut off the creature's tail and stuffed it into the pipe. A local trick, he said. My agony eased with a single drag. I asked him where I could get more and he led me to a hole in the cement wall, where we fished out several scorpions from the cobwebs, and I tried the old-school move, making them sting me twice, three, four times, right into the vein, until my toes went numb and my ears started to buzz.

The townspeople had never seen anything like it. They crowded around me, curious, and that's when Rutilo appeared to tell them I was crazy, I wanted to die, I was suicidal. That I'd stick around forever and bring nothing but misfortune to the village and god knows what else. One of the men, drunk, pulled out a pistol and tried to talk me into playing roulette with the other suicidal guy in town, a loopy alcoholic who'd supposedly survived his third round against some other reckless losers. Everyone referred to him affectionately as Bonesy.

'But I don't think it'll last much longer,' the other guy told me. 'Something tells me he'll be passing down the nickname to you. Seems like you're gonna be Bonesy now, my man.'

And they carried on like that, the assholes, trying to egg me on, cajoling Bonesy to join the game. Poor Bonesy: I may be fucked up, but compared to him I'm a regular dynamo. The dude was in seriously rough shape. He just sat there at the bar in a red baseball cap, hollow-eyed, trying to hold back the tears that brimmed one by one in his swollen eyes and trickled down his sunken cheeks, and he took very tiny sips of beer, like halting kisses on a cold, indifferent nipple.

I heard them talking, but I stopped responding. People just don't get it. They don't understand that I'm not suicidal. I don't want to kill myself, I don't even want to die. I don't want anything at all − I haven't wanted anything for a long time. My desire's all dried up. I'm dead in life, that's all.

'Don't be selfish,' they urged me. 'There's money on the line. If you kill yourself, then at least give someone else a break. It's the least you can do.'

No thanks, I repeated, that's not really the point, and Rubí yelled at them to leave me alone, I was fucked-up enough already, there was no point in mocking me on top of everything else. Chachi tried to rein in Beto, who was heating up for another fight, and Uriel wept and moaned, barely conscious. Silently, I swore to myself that I'd never go outside again, that the four cracked concrete walls of my rented room would become my living grave. There couldn't be much time left. There couldn't be much left of life to see; I'd seen it all, pretty much.

That's how the rest of the night and probably much of the early morning went: shouting, tears, lamentations. I managed to finish a second beer and felt the subtle vertigo of the alcohol and the *ba-bum ba-bum ba-bum* of my heart banging against my chest with the hit of meth I took. I felt a fiery tingling in my fingertips, my palms, and the soles of my feet, inside my nostrils and around my eyeballs, from all the scorpion venom I'd mainlined. People hollering over the thunderous trumpets and accordions, the interrogation lighting, the ambient smells of perfume mixed with beer and vaginal infections, smoke and cold ash, days-old sweat festering on the seats and walls − I could feel it all overwhelming my nervous system, which was growing less and less numb, less and less able to deal with the ruthless sensory overload.

I don't really remember the final stretch. Just that as an endless rotation of people stopped by our table, I caught some glimpses of my friend Mike and my girl

Valerie. They always show up when it's time to make a date with the lady. Rubí and Beto ignored them, but I remarked that Val looked better than the last time I saw her, when she was all blue and grey, her radiant eyes all dried out. She was so beautiful, I told them, but that time it was like picking up a wilted flower. They'd all been crying for a while, taking turns, but now Rubí hugged me and wept with real feeling. I have to go, I told them. I have to catch up with my wife.

'No problem, go ahead,' Chachi said. 'Don't you worry, she's definitely waiting for you where you're going. We'll all see each other there, if that's where we're all headed, I mean. Some of us just take longer to make the trip. You be careful not to get stuck along the way, got it? Better not get stuck as you finish your business. But don't worry, buddy, we'll see you when we get there, okay...'

Mike and Valerie came over and said it was time to go, that at the very least we should leave the bar and take a hit, or do a line, minimum. It bothered me to leave all those sad, lonely people behind, but I saw Val making her way out and I told everyone I'd be back soon. I followed, but no matter how hard I looked, I couldn't find her. Even so, I ducked into a vacant lot near the cantina and snorted just a little lady, and then just a little more. And I didn't go back inside after that. I have vague memories of staggering back to my room through the village, at a pale, tentative hour when the darkness, the silence, and the loneliness in the air feel exactly the way they felt when I'd first gone out, hours before, maybe days.

I think it was night-time when I reached my room. I smoked some opium and snorted some more lady as I cooked myself a fix. Then I got into bed and shot up and everything finally went back to normal at last.

6

I think I've pulled it off. There's nothing left: no presence, no awareness. I'm floating in a dark amniotic sea when I hear banging on the door. Just like every other time: slow at first, then louder and louder until it feels like they're going to kick it in. I leap up with enough time to wonder if it might be best to go shoot up in the jungle, so the ants can devour my bones before I manage to wake up, but I stumble to the door and open it.

It's my landlord, Don Tomás. He's come to ask if I'm staying, and to collect his money, because I've been here for ten days already, he says, and how much more am I going to pay him. I don't think it's an opium dream, although it's exactly the kind I get. I have no way of knowing how much time has passed and suspect the Don is lying. Probably shouldn't argue, though, if I want to avoid getting kicked out. I give him five hundred pesos so he'll put up with me for a few more days. He tries to peer into the room, but I block his view. He looks at me with disgust, like I'm just another piece of trash in the towering heap he'll have to haul out when my work there is done. He almost says something else, but he stops himself – he's better off accepting the five hundred pesos and whatever other sum he might milk from me if I last a couple more days on earth.

In the end, all he says is 'Well, hurry up with your business, then, 'cause we'll need the room for the maid.'

Once he's gone, I take stock of what I have on hand: eight hundred pesos, a little lump of opium – enough for maybe three good naps – and a couple of grams of lady. It's all melting away, but I'm still around. Sometimes I forget that I'm in a bit of a rush to carry out my mission here. I can't figure out how the money and the smack keep evaporating, but then it occurs to me that if I'm still alive, it's probably because I've been shooting up for days, and I must have eaten something over the past week. I must have smoked some cigarettes, and my body must have executed a series of actions on autopilot, though I can't remember any of them at this point.

I sit at the edge of the bed for quite a while, waiting for my brain to rev up again. I remember going to a bar, the scorpion stings, the gun they kept urging me to shoot myself with. Which doesn't seem like such a bad idea now. The rest is a blur. My lapses are getting worse. I hold my head in my hands for a long time, hunched over, paralysed. There's an overturned water jug with a little water at the bottom, a few cans of tuna and beans, some yogurt, and packets of noodle soup piled up in a corner of the bedroom, all swarming with ants and larvae. There are dribbles of wax and dozens of cigarette butts scattered all over the floor. Everything is coated in a thick film of ash, and the room smells of sickness and cold smoke. The Saint Jude votive candle has melted all the way down, but I seem to have ventured out for provisions: there are new candles, lighters, and matches, cotton, rum. The syringes are in a deplorable state; clearly I haven't managed to get any new ones.

Images and memories churn forth from the murky waters of my mind. Some can't be real, can't be anything but opium reveries. I know there's no way I could've headed into the jungle, toward the haciendas, because I would never have made it out. All of this has to be the dusky dream of a dying man. I think I spent several days wandering through town, but I remember almost nothing. Just scenes, flashes of myself drifting around El Zapotal, hungry, buck naked. Stray dogs trailed me, watching, and seemed to say, 'Hey, look, there goes Bonesy. Let's follow him and see what he's up to.'

I remember reaching what looked like an abandoned farm, searching for water, and coming upon a pen of scrawny cows. I remember squeezing mud into my mouth for the water to moisten my throbbing throat, chewing at brittle, porous earth. I remember a teenage girl with a bucket finding me and screaming her head off, and in the ensuing chaos an older man drove me off the plot with a machete. I remember he took pity on me at the gate and gave me a blanket, and he sat me down beneath a light bulb that flickered faint yellow light, and he asked his wife for a plate of rice and beans, which I ate without a word before I lurched my way back into the twilight.

I have no idea when these things actually happened. I've been dragging a lot of time behind me. I know my memories are linked and blended together somehow, that they've delivered me into this muffled, feverish moment, but I'm finding it harder and harder to distinguish experience from dreams.

I couldn't tell you when my body last expelled excrement. Maybe not since I got to El Zapotal. There's no movement in my intestines, not a rumble. The only bodily pulse I feel, beyond the faintness of my heartbeat, is the burn in my left arm, right here, where I shoot up. I swear they put something in this stuff to make it eat away at you. All the surrounding muscle goes numb and weak and goes to mush, and once you've shot up lots of times in the same place, the sores ooze and stink and take longer to scar.

I feel my veins course with a searing, unsettling fatigue, and I'm very hot. I'm not sure if it's the tropical climate, or the symptoms of some equatorial fever, or if my poisoned pipes are registering the onset of a sepsis that no one in town will be able to treat. I must weigh a hundred pounds, hundred and ten tops. I must be getting closer. I'm surprised by how stubbornly my body insists on staying alive despite how weak I've become.

With almost no money left, I'll be forced to sell my body to buy more smack, and scrounging up even the shittiest opium seems unthinkable. There can't possibly be a market for lady in this town. If there were, heroin would have infested it ages ago, would have devoured the entire population. There'd be nothing but empty houses with dry grey corpses slumped in bed, flopped on couches, slouched in armchairs facing still-illuminated TV sets, needles skewering their arms. No, there's definitely no dope around here – that's how far from everything we are. I'd have to travel to the nearest city, and to do that I'd have to whore myself out many, many times, and I'm sure I'll go into withdrawal halfway there, get the shakes and sweats. I'll start yelling, convinced that everyone wants to kill me or lock me up. If that happens to me way out in the middle of nowhere, I'd rather someone shoot me. I can't let myself get to that point.

7

I've reached a crossroads in my life. It's time for a drastic change of strategy. So I'm taking the measures I planned for this kind of situation: I've prepared myself an opium pipe and I'm getting into bed to smoke.

There's nothing more pleasurable than an opium nap. It's especially helpful in my case, because it instantly makes me more lucid, and I remember everything I forget when I'm awake. It's as if I were living a whole parallel existence on this cot, and the very smell of opium brings me back there. Its sweet bakery smell numbs my throat and sinks me into that warm, velvety place. I take several drags while I can still control my limbs, before they become foreign to me. Things take on a special sheen, an inner glow that grants them a muted breathing just like mine, just like my heartbeat, which becomes almost imperceptible. I feel a glint of vitality inside me, more or less like what I feel shooting through the metal bowl, the painting on the wall, the leg of the chair. My flesh grows indistinguishable from the matter that makes up all these things, and my spirit is unleashed from it, free to roam through time and space.

I see a valley forming by the seaside, and a red car winding through it along a dirt road, trailing dust and sand. I study the clarity of the scene, as if I'm inside it, before I realise that I've been here before. It was the time Cleto and Jairo and I went to the coast to get some lady. We were nineteen, and we'd finished a ball of opium the size of an orange, ten thousand pesos of pure fun that had to last us three months – but we were cleaned out in ten days. Meanwhile, our dealer had vanished and we were forced to go cold turkey. It was hell. We went out and wandered the slums, scared and sweaty and cold, but we never scored anything, so we got into Cleto's car and headed straight for the coast. I can still see Jairo's mohawk and split tooth, smiling even then. I can hear him say it'll be easy on the coast, that's why gringos go on holiday there, you can't miss it, you can get it right there on the beach from the coconut guy. But we never found any opium. Just the lady. None of us had ever tried it, but all we wanted was to feel better. And we sure did.

The first time you do heroin, you feel like you've finally found something extraordinary, something worth living for. We'd never had anything like that. Our lives were lonely and unremarkable until we met our lady. Then it was like we'd hooked up with the hottest woman on earth. It gave us a reason to never leave. You feel active, vigorous, like everything comes easy to you. You feel like the most charismatic guy at the party, the sharpest, the sexiest. It expanded the range of feeling at our disposal, way beyond the options available to mere mortals, whom we started to view with contempt. You're happy on H, as if you know exactly what you need. You do things with such ease and enthusiasm that afterwards you feel like you can't do anything without it ever again. You start to think that life without it isn't even life, just a tangle of pain and discomfort. An obstacle course. Real life, though not many people realise it, is life lived under the influence of the great señora.

It's nice to feel that you can solve all your troubles three times a day. Your misery gets worse and worse, it gets unbearable, but the solution gets simpler and simpler, too. You leave behind everything you know and dive into that world. And being there, you understand, comes at a price so high that few are willing to pay it. But you are, and you think your willingness grants you a kind of nobility, makes you a member of another species, and it's true. You do become a member of another species. In the end, you make the leap, because you think the reward will be worth it.

In the silken, sumptuous world of opium, I feel like I've come home, like I've been restored to an ancient, legendary place that was intimately familiar to me a long time ago. I feel the closeness of ornate ceilings, low domes enveloping me like a cocoon, and I delight in the faces of my friends all around me, because I know they're right there with me in this voluptuous hall. This place where all my wishes come true is mine alone, and here, just like this, is how I'm supposed to be, it's what I deserve. I know I'm gifted, aristocratic, and I feel blue blood running through my veins, so low in oxygen that it's nearly purple. The faces that surround me are beautiful, friendly, and they behold me with warmth and affection, even admiration.

You feel like you're leaning back on a throne, gazing out onto a vast, fertile landscape, and everything in sight belongs to you. It's the panorama of your mind, and you can fully inhabit it for a while, without anything to disturb your peace. You perch on the throne and regard your kingdom and you're satisfied. Any monster that tried to devour you would find nothing but air, an immaterial, ungraspable substance. You could reach enlightenment, utter fulfilment, if it weren't for the itch you feel as soon as the flash is gone, and you become mortal again: a small, fragile being made of squishy stuff that cramps and flails. It's a blessing to realise that it's not hard to return, that the road home is already mapped.

Then the effect would wear off and Cleto and I would turn to look at each other, and one of us would smile and say: 'One more?'

It was like asking a kid if he wants another ice-cream cone, another ride on the roller coaster. In the instant we'd spend smiling at each other before we responded, we weren't actually doubting whether to do it or not. It was just to reconcile ourselves with the futility of the decision, and maybe to create the illusion of having debated it at all.

'Sure, one more.'

And that's how we spent our days on the beach, sniffing smack. Jairo fell asleep in the sun and got completely charred, covered in second-degree burns. He looked like a walking piece of pork crackling, but he refused to go to the doctor. He cured the scorch with H. When we asked him why he hadn't got out of the sun, he said he just felt like he was getting deliciously cooked. In hindsight, it was a repulsive trip. We spent the whole time in roach-infested bedrooms, puking, getting bitten by mosquitos and sand fleas, applying white vinegar to Jairo as his skin shredded off like a chunk of slow-roasted pork. Even so, I can only remember us smiling. All the time. That was our first go, and I like to relive it because there was never anything like it ever again. That time on the beach with Jairo and Cleto, that's the feeling I've been chasing for years and never found, the home of mine I'm never going back to, a place I can only catch a hazy glimpse of now, from a great distance.

A few months later, Jairo died on us and Cleto was sent off to the countryside. That was the last I saw of him. Nothing went back to normal after that. People hear you're doing heroin and they act bewildered and defensive, as if you were trying to shoot *them* up. Personally, I think it's because they're curious, and it makes them nervous to know you have it on hand. God forbid you should tempt them or something. You say heroin and it's like you said anthrax or whatever. You say it's your lady and they want to burn you like a witch.

They're really nice to you at first, coaxing you to take the bait. They say you're special and unique, and they're going to treat you like you deserve, and when you start to think that maybe you could stand to enjoy the methadone they give you for breakfast, that's when the claws come out. They lower your dose, make you sit still, get all up in your business, and if you don't want to talk, they scream at you and lock you away. It's modern technology, but the method's still medieval. Only later do you learn that methadone withdrawal is worse than from heroin, and it lasts for months. Give me a fucking break. Months of shitting your pants and having the flu all the time. You realise they got you hooked on that shit just to keep you on a short leash, so you couldn't make a run for it even if you wanted to.

I'm certain that the visions of hell you see in museums were invented by someone who'd gone cold turkey. It's a fanfare of rancid fluids seeping from your every pore, accompanied by unbearable cramps and stinging, shooting pains and burning aches all over your body. And hallucinations: even the nurses look grotesque. It's terrifying, the pleasantness and benevolent air they torture you with. I've never moaned like I moaned in that place, never felt that kind of pain. So you break, and you cave, and you start to tell them whatever you think they want to hear.

They decide you're crazy and then it's like you're shoved into a meat grinder; you know you're never getting out of there in one piece, they won't rest until they strip you of your fat and ligaments and bones, and all that's left of you is a scrap of clean red meat. Therapy never did it for me. They say you do drugs to get your dad's attention, because you need love, because deep down you're looking for your mother.

'Bro, is this for real?' I'd tell them. Look, there's no way you're going to force-feed me the sexual frustrations of some old Viennese cokehead and convince me that's my cure. What I've got is called life, and nothing can cure me of that but the stuff I was shooting up five minutes ago. If the old fart had been doing heroin, they'd be giving me a prize right now. They say doing drugs is no way to live, because it kills you slowly – but life kills you slowly, buddy, and I'd rather live mine like this. You tell them they're a bunch of inhumane fascist pigs and they tell you the doors are wide open, nobody's keeping you there. You go back to the life that awaits you outside, it's your call.

So I grabbed my shit and left.

I fell back into my lady's arms, and to sleeping on friends' couches sometimes, although that never lasted for long. Parents weren't crazy about me. None of them ever said, 'Sure, stay the night, have some food, we won't judge you here, we'll support you. You can stay as long as you need.'

I would have been grateful. I would have told them, 'Thanks, ma'am, your living room's the perfect spot for shooting up ye olde H.'

There was nowhere else to go but the vestibules of familiar buildings, their rooftop terraces, a handful of parks, the stoops of closed shops. That's how it was for a while. I can still see the city streets, the damp dark avenues I roamed with the sickness for entire days and nights. I remember the presence of people lighting votive candles beside me as I slept on the pavement. I don't know if those people were real, because the dope was already dissolving my brain by then, I often saw people and things that weren't there, and I couldn't even look at a wall without the shifty silhouettes of skulls and demons rising up from the patterns in the cement. It's a relentless nightmare, withdrawal is, and the only thing that quells it is the lady. I can instantly feel my heart calming down, and I hear myself telling it, 'Easy, little guy, what's the rush? Time for your daily siesta…' The walls stiffen back into solid objects, the gates of hell swing shut, and the world stops being so sinister and tumultuous, at least for a little while.

Some people got me out of there. They scared me at first, because they looked like lepers or survivors of an atomic explosion; it was like something was eating away at their skin. I'd follow them hesitantly down dark alleys towards places that could barely be described as abandoned buildings. They were basements that smelled of death where people shed pieces of themselves: clothes, mattresses, syringes, blood and cum smeared across the floor, on the walls, shit amassed in buckets that no one had emptied for months. No one took out the trash, no one could even lift themselves up; they'd become part of the landscape. They even scattered their desires there, their ardours and ambitions, which festered from their bodies as they lay sprawled, cadaverous, to the point that you could feel the viscous, ethereal substance of all those people's hopes and dreams when you too lay down on the floor or leaned against a wall.

You come to wonder how anyone could live there. But they welcomed you, cooked you up a fix by candlelight. There's no generosity like the generosity of an addict easing the syringe out of his own vein to jab yours. When you feel the kick, and the torment you've been carrying around starts to dissipate at last, you look at them again and it's like you can see straight through the cloudy film over their eyes, the parched, cracked shell of their skin. It's like you truly see them for the very first time, and they're just like angels underneath. Their faces are supernaturally beautiful; they glow from within. Their eyes receive you with a divine stillness, like what some people call mercy. Then you understand why they live there. This place you've come to is the warmest and most welcoming on earth.

It's been a long time since I've felt accompanied by a presence as benevolent as what I felt then. I get these glimmers of close, kind company, smells that bring me back to distant times. I keep following the trail of the sweet, the soft, the cosy, right back to that dead end, and I always run into my Valerie along the way. My punk princess, elegant and refined. When I smoke opium, she appears as vividly as if she were still alive. I remember her skin, inked with sea monsters and dagger-pierced tongues, a treasure map. And she was the treasure, a mystery I didn't ever want to solve.

Lost eras return to me like mirages, but I see everything from the outside, detached as a ghost. I relive the wild, terrible times we spent together, the dramas on the stairs of her building, her uncontrollable tears and screaming when she found out I was with the lady instead of her. But she always came back, loving me more urgently than ever, as if she knew our time together was running out. Val never liked heroin, but she knew there was no other way for us to be together, so she set out on this journey too. And she outstripped me. When I smoke opium and see her in my dreams, she isn't sad or angry. It's not that she's waiting for me, because she's no longer fettered to the laws of time. She observes me from a distance. Maybe she's touched to see me struggling to catch up with her.

I sense my dog Kid in a corner of the room, as if he were right there, licking my hand, circling me, growling and whining, waiting for the rush to pass so I'll take him out. Poor Kid; he probably spent most of his life needing to pee. I see him in front of me, just like when he was still a puppy. I remember I showed up at the cave and Mike was playing with him. 'Flaco, check this out, we found you a dog,' he said as I came in. 'See? He looks just like you.'

Poor Kid was scrawny, battered, and slick with motor grease. He did look just like me. I kept protesting and complaining, but by then the dog had started following me everywhere with his hungry orphan eyes. I hear his insistent whimpers in the background. Kid was the smartest dog in the world. He outfoxed everyone. He learned to sniff out heroin and could always find the dealers when we went out on the prowl. If we took a little on the train, he'd wake us up before we missed our stop. Which we often did, if we ignored him. My favourite thing was how happy he was just to flop down next to you, to keep you company as the rush passed, and all he wanted in return was that you give him a scrap of food and take him out to piss. I think you could search the whole world over and never find a friend like that, like the friend I had back then.

Still drowsy, I cook myself a fix and take a few drags of opium. The lady draws out the opium visions. I slip into a deathlike state and let myself be hypnotised by the spectacle of lights inside my skull. I've spent entire weeks this way, prostrate on a mattress, practising not ever getting up again, feeling how the walls close in on me until they press right into my chest. My ears ring with an electric murmur, like a waterfall or a high-tension cable. But the sounds of the village seep in through my window, and even in my stupor, I know everything: I hear dog barks and church bells, heavy footfalls on the road, deadly brawls and livid weeping in the aftermath. I hear funeral processions and moans of pain and pleasure that issue from people's houses at any time of day. I remember what happens when I'm on the other side of the smoke: the dead return, or maybe I go to the place where the dead live, and they let me stay with them for a while.

Yes, heroin is a portal to the world of the dead. Because it kills you slowly, and there's no such thing as a life of doing heroin, just a gradual descent into the underworld. But also because, when you mainline lady, your whole metabolism slows down. A kind of silence spreads inside you, and you hear the dead, you feel them around you. You hear them whispering, feel their inquisitive stares.

The dead observe us with a mix of fascination and utter detachment. Most are no longer involved in earthly affairs. I think they must feel pity and tenderness towards us because we still are, because of how seriously we take everything. They see it all as if from behind a glass window, from the perspective of someone who no longer has anything at stake, no more obstacles to overcome, not even time itself.

Some don't want to be dead. They want to keep playing at life, and since they can't, they get anxious, wandering restlessly through the world, hounding the living. This town is full of them. They come and go in the streets, the halls of people's houses; they sneak inside to watch. It's best to tune them out, because when they realise you can see them, they take an interest in you as well. They come in and sit down on my bed or stand in the doorway, and they talk to me, because they know I can hear them, that even though I'm still here, on this side, I'm really one of their own. They tell me their worries, send me on errands, make requests: 'Please, I beg you, go see my cousin and tell him to forgive his compadre for what happened with that woman who tricked him. If you see him passed-out drunk, grab the gun he keeps on the stovetop and toss it into the jungle. That rifle belonged to my uncle, and my uncle will be sad if he uses it to kill his godson. Tell my cousin that none of them will ever rest: not him, not his compadre, not my uncle, either. Please go tell him before he does something he shouldn't, I'm begging you...'

That's the drill with them. And I tell them no, it's none of my business, I've come looking for peace, if I get caught stealing firearms I'll get strung up and lynched. I'm no good for that kind of job.

'But you're on your way out. What is it to you? Do something good before you go, don't be selfish.'

Even the dead try to take advantage, even when you're basically just peeling away in bed, slowly crumbling into dust, useless beyond providing a shoulder to cry on.

Another time, a little girl came into the room. At first I thought she was a girl from town. She was maybe nine and crying about a dog.

'Have you seen my dog?' she asked. 'He ran across the highway and I ran after him but I can't find him anywhere.'

I pretended to be asleep, but the girl pestered me until I opened my eyes a crack and lifted my head.

'No, little girl, your dog's not here.'

She sucked in her snot and rubbed her eyes. 'Where's my doggie?' she whimpered.

'Your dog left with the light,' I tell her. 'You should go there too. That's where you'll find him.'

She lingered for a while, stubborn, sniffling, tugging at my arm. I don't know if she paid any attention to what I said, but eventually she left. To keep looking for her dog, I guess.

It's happened a bunch of times. When I wake and sit up in bed, I can still remember them: who they were, what they'd come to tell me. They're all trapped in a kind of loop: time passes, but they insist on doing the same things over and over. They go looking for help, and as soon as they find someone, they start begging and whining, because they think you'll take pity on them and bend over backwards to help.

One of them shows up and says, 'Take off my socks, please. I never wore yellow socks in my whole life. My children put them on me out of spite. Please, I'm begging you. Go to the cemetery and take off these damned socks.'

After a while, another one comes in: 'Listen, I need you to go find my farm. Antonio Sierra, at your service. Tell my wife I buried a box of silver charms under the fig tree. I tried to tell her, but I was paralysed, so I couldn't. Tell her I sent you, and that she should give you the emerald pendants in return... please, go, go...'

Later, another: 'Come on, give me a little money for a beer, man, don't be cheap. I was on my way home when some thugs beat me up. All I want is to have one little drink to calm my nerves. I keep asking and asking and no one wants to help a guy out. Have a heart, man.'

I sit in bed for a long time, thinking, smoking one cigarette after another. I'm not new to this stuff. I know the deal. I know the drug doesn't just numb your brain, but contaminates it, gnaws away at it, wears it down. I've seen it happen countless times. People start hallucinating, they think the house has been invaded by bugs, they feel ants crawling all over their skin, larvae wriggling in their bellies. Then they start seeing everyone they left along the way. You see them just sitting there, talking to themselves. If they don't off themselves quickly, they end up raving and drooling, writhing in bed, so incapacitated that they can't even get up to take a shit. Their nerves are fritzed into some kind of weird rubber pulp.

I think a lot about my friend Elisa's brother. They called him Christ, for fuck's sake; his name must have been Christopher. One of my earliest memories of that dude was his bedroom ceiling: the whole thing was spattered brown, because whenever he hit an artery while shooting up, his blood would spurt all over the place. By the time I met him, he was close to finishing the paint job. The guy's blood got infected and the bacteria started eating away at his heart valves. Who knows how many millions of heroin shots it cost dear Elisa's parents to keep him alive, but the fact is they fixed up his heart, and then he kept shooting up anyway, so the infection came back.

Poor old Christ ended up in an aseptic room. Since the infection was raging uncontrollably, and they had to keep cutting him open to operate or inject him with antibiotics, they decided there was no point in even sewing him up any more. He was laid out on a surgical bed in his bedroom, totally conscious, with his chest wide open and his heart exposed. You could see it beating and everything. Even he could peer inside and get a glimpse if he craned his neck a little. They gave us some face masks and let us go in, supposedly to say goodbye, although it was mostly meant to scare us. Because, let's face it, the dude was fucking scary. Even with his whole fucking heart uncovered and the inside of his chest laid bare, he'd still smile and make small-talk with you. He'd show off all the drugs they were pumping into him every second of the day, mostly to keep him calm, because whenever so much as a glimmer of lucidity hit him, he'd freak out and beg you to please just kill him and get it over with. But there was nothing to be done. His parents wanted to save him. They wanted him alive, end of story.

That's how they kept him for days, maybe weeks. After a while, of course, the poor kid started sort of losing his mind. He fixed the ceiling with that beatific smile of a junkie mid-rush, as if receiving visions from another dimension. He greeted us one by one, even those of us who weren't there any more, and went on about all the opulence and finery around him, how there was only silence everywhere and from the silence emanated the voices of people taking care of him, and we thought he was talking about his aseptic room. I'll never forget old Christ chatting away and weeping, his face contorted, his whole heart on display. The guy looked like some twisted Nazi experiment. In the end it was hard to tell if he was alive or just sort of re-animated – if he was really the one moaning and thrashing, or if it was just his body still flailing there. Who knows what kind of debt he owed to end up all split open and put on display like that. They didn't even let him keep his own meagre, ruined heart in the privacy of his chest.

I realise the drugs have liquefied my brain, that I can't trust what I see and hear. I know I'm incapable of distinguishing opium dreams from real life, and it's ridiculous to think I can actually talk with the dead. But the more I dwell on it, the more sense it makes. I'm so close to becoming one of them that the border between us grows wispy, frail. Maybe it sometimes fades away altogether. It's been happening to me for a while. It's just hard for me to remember when I'm awake. It's like I've already joined them, already turned into a spirit doggedly clinging to the corpse it drags along.

It can't be the first time a junkie has developed the ability to see the dead. It must have happened to Christ, and it must happen to the elderly and the terminally ill, to patients anaesthetised on operating tables and people trapped in collapsed buildings or fires. It's a little-known phenomenon, because once we're that close to the threshold, our minds are under such painful pressure that we can't really understand what's coming over us. Our bodies are unable to speak, or there's no one left in our lives to tell us what's happening. No one listens, and if they do, they think we're crazy. Our faculties last as long as this liminal, transitory state itself, the frontier that separates us from the void. And soon we're dead, too. Then there's nothing else to tell or anyone to tell it to. That's why I want to tell it here, while I still can.

It crosses my mind that at some other point, with a little more vitality and ambition to spare, I could've taken advantage of all this. A necromancer with a knack for mediating between the dead and their families – that sounds like a pretty lucrative profession in this kind of town. I could've charged for entrance to a tent where I'd bring the living into contact with their loved ones and solve the problems tormenting restless souls, not to mention their descendants. All with the added benefit that, unlike the unsettling phantasmagorical spectacle concocted by most circus mediums and third-rate witch doctors, mine wouldn't be a scam. I might have come to be a man of status and power in El Zapotal, a respectable gent that families hope will marry their daughters in thanks for an invaluable resource. A man the village loves and supports and provides for, lest he take off for another town and offer his services elsewhere.

On the other hand, who knows if all my visitors are real. Maybe it's just another way of going crazy. My own way. There's just one way to know for sure: I have to go find the farm owned by this Antonio Sierra guy and see if he really did bury a box of silver charms under a fig tree. There's no reason why I should, other than to prove my own theory and show I'm not insane. And also because I'll be running out of lady soon, and if I have to retreat to a city for more, I'd better figure that out in advance.

That said, I'll probably have crossed the border by then, perched in my lady's little boat. I know I'll make it across: no one stays put unless they have unfinished business on this side, and I don't have anything at stake any more. Only this. I want to make sure the whole thing isn't a hallucination, because it would make my mission here more meaningful. I'd know for sure that I'm a real visionary, almost a saint, not just a junkie at a dead end. I think it'd do me some good to go out, maybe for the last time – to leave this dump where I've been cooped up for days, a room that's started to take on the dusty, corroded look of a crypt. Maybe a smidge of physical exertion, a bit of air and sunlight will be enough to do me in. There'll be plenty of time for the grave, and if I turn out to be right, then maybe I can even make a little money – who cares how little – off this whole shitty situation. At the end of the day, that's what matters to me: I can't run out of smack. And who the hell cares about being a man of status, loved and respected, in a place like El Zapotal?

8

It's been a long time since I've managed to control the part of my mind that takes logical decisions, although I know it still exists. I know I've still got some reason in me, I just don't really know what governs it. Maybe there's more than one kind of reason. Sometimes I get the sense that there are two people inside me: one – the one I identify as 'me' – trying to extinguish itself, which means shedding the weight of matter by using the quickest, most painless methods at his disposal, and another one, far more stubborn and vicious and evasive, who stays alive in spite of everything and drags me around wherever he goes.

My decision-making process involves a violent confrontation between these two sides of my personality. This means that even the simple act of going to the kitchen and washing a mug can take me entire days, but contriving and executing an elaborate con to get my hands on a gram of horse can take me twenty minutes, no matter the obstacles. It's weird that both sides can reach an agreement and take anything remotely resembling a decision. But when they do, I always find out when it's already too late, when I'm all dressed up and wandering around like a resuscitated corpse, perfectly aware of where I'm going but lacking any notion of how I got there.

I ended up walking the streets of a godforsaken town, bound for the farm of a man I'm not sure even exists. I don't need the silver charms, because the engine in my chest is on the verge of cutting out. Don Tomás, or whoever finds me, can use them to pay for a proper burial, or maybe – this is much more likely – he'll keep them as compensation for the trouble of dealing with my body when I'm gone. All I know for sure is that, if my remaining smack doesn't kill me, the charms will grant me a margin of error, an escape hatch in case my plan fails.

It's hard to get directions around here. People always avoid me, scattering when they see me coming, and I struggle to move quickly enough to catch up with them. I raise my voice and call out, but it's like they're all deaf. I dragged my feet along the dusty, pitted roads in the punishing heat. My body wanted to sweat, but it was all out of water, and so my flesh burned as if coated in open sores. I studied the cracked skin of my hands, my ragged clothes. Everything about me seemed to be falling apart, trailing a fine wake of greyish dust. I could hear the horseflies hovering around the ivy on one side of the street, but beyond it was utter silence, as if time had stood still. I knocked on the doors of a few adobe and tin-roofed houses, tugged the cords of bells that clanged inside the ranches, but no one came. I spied the church in the distance and thought my best bet would be to walk in that direction. It was a long walk and I didn't feel up for such a trek, but my feet obeyed, one after the other, and I kept going.

I followed the path and sensed presences all around me. When I stopped to look, I couldn't see anything moving at all. I thought I caught a glimpse of some kids in rags, tracking me from the underbrush, but I soon lost sight of them. After a little while, I saw the silhouette of a man heading towards me on the road, talking to himself. He looked preoccupied, engrossed in his troubles. He was rubbing his neck, his shoulders, his back, and as he approached, I heard him say 'Oh dear… my back… my back hurts so much…'

Then he looked up and saw me. I walked on. He neither shrank back nor startled, just stood there staring, and then he spoke: 'Sorry, there's no one behind me, is there?'

We were the only people in sight.

'No, sir, no one at all.'

'Ugh, I keep feeling like there's something behind me,' he said, and craned his neck as if to peer over his shoulder or scratch his back, 'that burns like a mother…'

This had to be the town madman. I would have rather avoided him, but it wasn't like I had loads of other people to ask, so I went for it. 'Sorry, which way is Antonio Sierra's farm?'

He stared as if he had no idea what I was talking about. 'You're going the wrong way,' he said. 'The cemetery's over there.' He gestured in the opposite direction.

'I'm not going to the cemetery,' I said.

He smiled as if I were teasing him. 'That's where we're all headed.'

The guy seemed perplexed. I think he thought I was dead. He could have paid closer attention. Folks must be very used to them around here.

I kept walking.

'Excuse me,' he said, 'do you know how much the crossing costs?'

I stopped short again, puzzled. 'To where?' I asked. 'Do you really have to pay to walk around this place?

He stared and laughed, then clapped a hand over his

mouth as if he'd said too much. 'My goodness, you're more lost than I am, aren't you? Or maybe it's not your turn yet.'

The man drew closer as he spoke, studying the track marks on my neck, my arms. He was covered in dirt, and ants swarmed over his face and hands, crawling out from under his sleeves. He came so close that he could practically smell me, the weirdo, before he blurted, 'I brought them the eyes of my wife Fabiola, but they refused. Now I'm going back for the hands of Venus Ochoa, the bastard who stole her from me. I'm going to use them to scratch my back. That's what I want most in the whole world. You think they'll take them?'

I met his wild eyes with unease, but I didn't answer. This was no normal lunatic. He was one of those angry ghosts, the kind who goes looking for revenge. It hit me even before he turned to go, when I saw the three lentil-sized bullet holes riddling his back. I stood frozen as he walked away. It took me a while to set out again. Then I trudged along the path for quite some time, under the sun, following the cross above the bell tower of the church that rose up from the distant hills.

At one point I stopped to focus on a rhythmic sound behind the cornfields, metallic and scratchy, and my feet instinctively carried me towards it. A half-dozen men were in a vacant lot, slashing at weeds with machetes that released a sharp note of thrumming steel as they struck the ground and clashed against the rocks beneath. These guys did seem made of flesh and blood. They stopped working as soon as they saw me, straightened up, and stared without a word. I walked closer so I wouldn't have to yell. All I could hear was the wind hissing in the grass. The men stood in silence, gripping their machetes and watching me, as if I were an apparition – but I got the sense that they knew exactly how to deal with one.

Once I was within range, I asked after Antonio Sierra's farm. Much to my surprise, it actually existed. One of the men, who was maybe sixty and had weathered skin and wore a straw hat, took a few steps forward and said yes, it was about two hundred metres away, crossing the stream and following a path that cut across a cactus field. And why did I want to know, he asked.

'You're awfully skinny to be from the bank.'

I said there was something I had to do at Señor Sierra's request. And how was that, the man replied, I was far too late, Toño Sierra had suffered an embolism six years prior and was unable to move or speak before his death two years after that. He'd left behind a daughter and his poor wife, and the bank was supposed to show up any day now to seize the property.

I thanked him and turned to go. It took me a while to get out of range, and I heard them jeering before they went back to work. Moving away from the steady slashing sound of the machetes, I continued on, propelled by a stubborn and unfamiliar force of will, towards Antonio Sierra's farm.

I took the path they'd told me about, struggling with every step to reach the stream, and every few metres I had to rest on a stump or boulder to catch my breath. It made sense that good old Toño Sierra had chosen me to bring his wife this message. Anyone else would have snuck into the farm, poisoned the dogs, dug a hole under the fig tree in the dark, and pilfered everything without a peep to the woman of the house. Or they would have waited for the bank to repossess the land, then left it deserted for a while, then come back to burrow in peace. I didn't have the strength, let alone the ambition. In that sense, I get it: in spite of everything, I'm still here, wandering around, though not for much longer now. I'm the perfect candidate. Some time back, I turned onto a one-way alley too narrow for U-turns. Nothing can keep me in this world any more, not even money, not even love. What kind of love could ever compare to what you feel for Death, who adores us like a mother, who's always ready to welcome us back into her womb? There's nothing that interests me more than smack at this point, and smack doesn't keep me here on earth. Instead, it's slowly driving me away.

But the flesh is stubborn. Soon enough I was crossing the stream and saw, a few metres away, the cactus field that marked the entrance to Antonio Sierra's farm. I took countless twists and turns of the path that snaked among the nopales, without a single tree in sight, a single shadow to seek shelter in. I kept walking, step by step, even when my brain had started to cook inside my skull and I thought I might pass out. I continued until I glimpsed the little white shack, encircled by a blue-painted wall hemming a well and a fig tree. Nearby were a couple of chickens, a plot of corn, and a rickety old pick-up. That was the whole farm.

The girl – she couldn't have been over twenty – received me at rifle-point. What did I want, what was I doing there. Her mother observed me warily from the threshold of the house. As soon as I set eyes on her, she seized a silver cross that hung from an oak-bead rosary around her neck, fingering it compulsively. Had I come from the bank to take the farm, the daughter asked, because if I had she'd blow my brains out right then and there, so I'd better hit the road. I tried to ask for a glass of water, but my voice sounded parched and raspy, like a groan or a death rattle. My throat burned when I swallowed. I could feel my brain pulsing in my temples, my eyes so dry and toughened that they were practically squeezing out of my head. When the women realised I was dying of thirst, the daughter lowered the gun and came closer, while the mother went out to the well. They sat me down in the shade and gave me a glass of water, then another. They thought I must be one of those anthropologist types who sets out in search of gold and ruins, that I'd spent months wandering lost in the jungle.

Some time passed before I was able to explain why I'd come. They didn't want me in the house, but eventually they couldn't take the sun any more and let me in as far as the living room, the daughter's watchful eyes scrutinising my every move. I passed a mirror hanging in the hall. I hadn't seen my reflection in weeks, and I couldn't have imagined what I found there. I was a skeleton clad in lacerated leather. The bags under my eyes could have been painted on with a thick coat of black grease. I looked as if I'd emerged from underground, as if I were already being devoured by insects that had second thoughts halfway through lunch.

I found Antonio Sierra on the living room sofa, staring into space, looking absent or catatonic. The women didn't see him: they invited me to sit down on top of him. No thanks, I said. So I just stood there, hunched, clutching my innards so as not to spit them out on the living room floor. Then I understood that Antonio Sierra, even in death, was still stuck on the couch, paralysed by his embolism. It had become a habit of his.

I explained the situation, telling them as concisely as I could manage that Antonio had left an inheritance and I could help them find it, that all I asked for in return were some silver charms set with emeralds that Antonio had promised me if I would do him this favour.

Mother and daughter exchanged suspicious glances. I knew what they were thinking: improbable and fantastical, my story reeked of fraud. It didn't help that the messenger was a filthy junkie on his last legs, although it did make sense, in a way: no one else could have done it. I wondered if I might be disrupting a delicate balance struck between the living and the dead, and I would almost have preferred it if they'd laughed in my face and sent me back to my cell, bent on shooting up my final fix of lady. But they didn't. What I told them had hit a nerve: they'd long wondered what Antonio had done with his money, meticulous saver that he was. Miser that he was, better put. They'd been looking. They were interested, they had nothing to lose. Before long, the daughter had come up with some picks and shovels and we gathered by the fig tree, ready to determine whether this hare-brained affair was even possible in our supposedly rational world.

I didn't expect they would make me dig, but they did. It was the gentlemanly thing to do, and the implicit message was that if I wanted those silver charms, I'd have to earn them. It's not every day that you get to behold the pathetic spectacle of a skeleton digging a hole. People forget how arduous and exhausting it is; I wasn't up to snuff. They gave me half a tortilla with beans and a slice of avocado, which was all that kept me from fainting on the spot. Don Antonio had done his job well: he didn't want the first rains of the season to unearth his treasure, and at half a metre down we still hadn't found a thing. There he stood the entire time, gazing vacantly into the horizon, silent.

Once we'd been at it for a while, it occurred to me that I could seize the opportunity to dig my own grave. That way, having fulfilled our mission of finding the treasure chest, I could ask the two women to drag me into the pit, give me my shot of lady, and bury me right there. Finding myself on the verge of collapse, the daughter took over for me. I sat nearby, listening to the girl as she dug, the shovel's rhythmic blow against the earth, until the heat and the sound began to soothe me. Exhaustion took over and I fell asleep in the shade of the fig tree. It was a deep, coma-like sleep, my body stiff and cramped from exertion.

Then my memory goes blank. It was much later when I woke. The sun had set and the sky was dense with grey clouds. I could hear the groaning of distant thunder, like hungry innards, and a thick steam rose from the ground, hot and stifling. I'd sensed a distant hubbub in my dreams, an ebb and flow of footsteps punctuated by brief, muffled shouts, breathing, and whispers, and once I was awake I struggled to lift my head and look around. I felt the two women staring at me, waiting for me to emerge from my stupor, coming and going behind my back, studying me with distrust and disapproval.

I tried to get up, but my body didn't want to follow suit. It felt almost dismantled to me, like a little wire doll or slack-stringed puppet – as if only the cracked hide that covered me was keeping my bones from scattering all over the place. When I lifted my head at last, I found myself utterly alone. I made my way towards the fig tree and crouched to peer into the hole, nearly a metre deep around the tree – which looked now like a patient who hadn't survived an operation, its roots exposed in an arterial tangle, splintered and useless. There was nothing but an empty pit in the earth, and the two women had vanished.

I dragged my numb body back to the house, which was locked and dark, as if abandoned for years. There were no hens, no pick-up. Even the corn plot looked more parched and neglected than it had seemed on first sight. I couldn't help but wonder if I'd slept for days, even months, if I hadn't finally died in my sleep. I circled the house, banging on doors and windows, but no one was in.

I thought they could have gone into town, or off to the nearest city to pay the bank, but no. They'd tricked me. They'd awaited my moment of exhaustion to make a break for it. If they turn up again, they'll surely be ready to lie, to deny everything. I may not look very physically imposing, but they must think I'm a lunatic, or a demon, that I want to take everything that's theirs. Or they fear that if the townspeople find out, someone will show up at their house to steal their jewels and slit their throats. They must be far away by now.

I called out to them, shouted as loudly as I could. 'Señora, for the love of God, all I want is to see if this is real, to make sure I'm not crazy. Please, I don't want to go crazy. I'm not long for this world, but I need this so I can leave in peace. Do it for me.'

I was horrified to hear my own voice begging and imploring. I was starting to sound like them – like a suffering soul. Sierra's widow must have thought that my life wasn't even worth the price of those silver charms, and she may very well have been right. In truth, I never really expected to earn anything. I only went because I wanted to understand what was happening to me. I pictured the woman and her daughter speeding out of town in the pick-up, the mother stroking the oak beads of her rosary. Maybe she was praying because she'd broken her husband's promise. But it didn't matter, because that night she'd pray harder and ask God's forgiveness, and now that they were going to have money, the rest would be water under the bridge, me included.

Warm thick drops of rain started tumbling from the sky, lifting dust, and my shirt was soon soaked through. I think I'd more or less kept my head held high until then, even when I had to drag my feet, but those times were gone. I crossed the plot – I wasn't so much walking as crawling by then – to a little gate set into the wall and pushed my way out. All I wanted was to get back to my room and see my lady, then rid myself of all the doubts I'd ever harboured, once and for all.

The rain intensified. My feet sank into the mud as I followed the dirt path, and the downpour was so fierce that I could barely see in front of me. My clothes were drenched, heavy on my bones, hunching my back even more than usual. I stopped for a moment, listening to the thunder, then stripped down: first my shoes, then my t-shirt, my trousers. The air was warm despite the rain. The water turned grey as it streamed over my skin, washing from my hair and forehead the dense film of dust that had gathered there with the passing days.

I felt a rush of rage – not because of the jewels or the deceit, but because of the uncertainty they'd condemned me to. Maybe this town really was forsaken by God. Now I also had to consider the chance that there was no treasure chest at all, that the whole business at the farm was just a hallucination, a fantasy I'd cooked up in an opium dream out of stuff I'd overheard at the bar, that the true ghosts were those men in the field who'd told me the farm did exist – or the two women claiming to be Antonio Sierra's wife and daughter.

I'm not sure if it was my exhaustion and weakness or the prickling onset of withdrawal, but I felt something there, as I took in the purple and orange light seeping through the clouds and the flashes of lightning that pierced the grey cloak of the sky. I was certain that my moment was near. It had taken far too long, and I felt good, too good, like a flame crackling with brilliant sparks as it burned through the final drops of fuel. My body was dying; soon it wouldn't be habitable any more.

It must have been the first time I really thought about it, because I felt a stab of anguish in my belly, like a child whose parents forgot him at the grocery store or at school. I felt poor, helpless, and I remember wondering where my home would be now, where I'd go for shelter later. At that moment, El Zapotal seemed like the worst place in the world to die. I felt like throwing up, but I didn't even have the strength to retch. Everything had atrophied. I squeezed out my clothes in the torrential rain, slung them over my shoulder with the kit in my pocket, and carried on my halting, cadaverous way, stark naked, towards my room.

I need to consider the possibility that I'm alone, really alone, on the verge of death in a ghost town – and delirious to boot, concocting fantasies to keep myself company, to feel like I could be of interest to someone. I'd better get used to the idea that for the first time, this enterprise I embarked on so many years ago – and will never return from – is starting to scare me a little. I no longer understand what's next. Maybe the ghosts can answer my questions, but Antonio Sierra is nowhere to be found. And even if he turned up, who knows if I could believe a word he said after everything that's happened to me.

A date with the lady: that's what's next. That I do know.

9

The rain had stopped by the time I reached my room, naked and soaked, my feet caked in mud up to the ankles. The sun was peeking through the clouds, the air had cooled and sharpened, and a warm orange light honed the edges of everything. I even saw a rainbow just before I reached my room. It was a perfect day to die. I stepped in, tossed my waterlogged clothes onto a chair, and sat on the concrete floor, still naked, to prepare my final act. I cooked it up and filled a needle with a strong dose, leaving nothing but residue in the can. I couldn't waste anything. It was dusk, and I was running late already.

I had the fix all ready to go in the needle. An electric blue light filled the whole room. I remember the syringe against my skin, which gleamed with sweat as if made of creased plastic, and beneath it my tired, toughened vessels, barely pulsing now. I can't remember exactly when I took the plunge, because I had a few hits of opium before that and sniffed the leftover lady in the can, and between the opium and the lady I always forget things, especially details.

I don't think I'd even emptied the whole syringe when I started to feel the rush, the tingle like a warm, damp animal, feather-soft, but powerful enough to snap your spine. I feel it crawling through my veins, invading my heart, and climbing my vertebrae, nibbling at everything in its path, cutting through my neck and into my brain, where something shattered inside me. I feel a release of energy that had lain dormant until then, a capacity for rapture, ecstasy. My whole body goes numb, as if enveloped in a hug so tight I can barely breathe or hear anything around me.

My thoughts unfurl before my eyes with total clarity; I follow their courses and conjugations until they fork into meandering paths I can no longer reconcile. Then I fall into a deep coma, floating away from a shore that thins and narrows in the distance as I hover in an all-enveloping void. I don't know if my eyes are open or shut, but I feel as if I've been packed into a narrow box, and I drop down into the darkest, farthest reaches of some underground realm. I'm not unfamiliar with the sensation of sinking; I've done it all my life. I know you never hit the bottom. Lying there, motionless, I sink and sink, and in the depths I find my memories, like monstrous creatures swimming in the ocean's darkest chasms.

There I see Valerie. I can feel her warm body embracing me, her slow breath on my neck, the tingle that wakes my skin into goosebumps when she strokes my back. I always felt so safe and at peace with her that I'd nod off in her arms, flooded with dreams and ideas, like when I smoke opium. I think it's the closest thing I've ever experienced to a shot of lady.

Peering through the waters, I see her body stretched out in bed. I catch her wildflower scent and glimpse a house, smoke curling out of a stone chimney, way up on a mountain slope, above the clouds. I see dogs and kids running among the trees, and I see my dead friends, older now, cooking meat on a grill. Impossible scenes.

Everything I could have ever longed for. I forgot about desires and pleasures long ago. That's what the lady does. She replaces all that stuff, and your life starts to revolve around your next date with her, nothing more.

I remember every single date with Valerie. They file through my field of vision like spectres or mirages, starting with the very first: Valerie at the bus station, refined as ever, sheer vitality. We had coffee and I warned her I'd be her downfall. She just laughed. I see other scenes too, like when I took her up to the rooftops downtown and to the railroad scrapyard. I always spoke honestly about what I was doing with my life, and I think she saw me as something like a rescue kitten: she picked me up, tried to nurse me back to health. She thought love could save me. Poor girl, she always did have a tragic streak. Some people seem born to suffer – their virtue and vocation. Valerie was always like that.

I don't know why we chose to fall in love, although who knows if you get to choose such things. I do know why I fell in love, even when I never expected that to happen, never thought a woman like Val could ever love me just as I was. I have no idea why she did. But she must have found a crack in my shell, because she got through to me, the only one to ever make it in. I think life tried to save me through Valerie. That's what I believe. I don't want to think it was sending her off to the incinerator, even if that's what happened in the end.

She used to say that the lady was like my lover, and I reassured her that she was the only one I loved. Over time, our dates had more and more to do with the lady than with each other, until she got hooked herself. We'd curl up like a pair of foetuses for days, and she started losing weight. But the circles under her eyes and the deathly look were beautiful on her. She was like a duchess of the night. All you wanted was to find the medicine so the porcelain doll would smile again, because when she finally did, it was like the sun came out, illuminating everything in sight. I remember our outings around the city, the times we'd shoot up and lie in the park together, or hole up in her apartment, before she lost the lease and moved in with me. I remember every date with her, my lady, except for the last one. There the visions stop, my memories tangle and disintegrate, the tingle of the lady starts to fade. Everything muddles together and is thrown back into chaos, and I can't reconstruct that last date. I think I may have stood her up. I feel like the same thing is about to happen, that I won't be able to catch up with her this time, either.

I feel a string pulled tight in me, then snap, and a brilliant light floods my eyes, as if someone had yanked out the final frame of a film roll. The celluloid starts to fog and bubble until it evaporates, leaving me floating in a milky neon liquid that swamps everything around me, and all I can hear is a static murmur, a tenuous tuning fork in the depths of a galaxy mid-fusion, millions of kilometres away. The first thing I feel is panic, as if I were suffocating. I try to kick my feet, shift my neck, move my arms, but I can't find them. My body is far, far away.

Before I get truly confused, peering into the white darkness I'm enveloped in, I glimpse a woman's form, and I feel something I never feel when I'm high: something akin to fear. I know I can't look her in the eyes, so I lower mine. I know that if I look up, the humming I hear could shatter me into a thousand pieces. Advancing from the edge of my vision, a dense darkness rises and threatens to swallow me whole. It's the way out, and it looks like a black hole consuming everything. I know I can't go there. Not because I'm afraid, but because I don't yet understand what's happening to me. I'd rather stay here, where I can still discern some shadows past the milky cloak of light.

A vague sense of mobility returns and intensifies. My body is starting to feel again. I feel like I'm being carried in a box from one place to another, sometimes vertically and sometimes horizontally: vast distances across the atmosphere or the earth's crust. I'm inserted into vaults, domes, glass walls cast with light fractals, each inhabited by a different entity. When I squint, I see bodies towering around me, massive presences with animal heads that observe me like an insect emerging from its chrysalis. I'm surrounded by colossal beings, as if laid out on an operating table. And it's clear that the prognosis is bad.

'How much longer will this last?' I ask them.

They exchange glances void of all emotion, then they examine me with their curious faces, some like crows, others like crickets, others like jackals.

'How much longer do you want it to last, flaco? It can last as long as you like.'

'We invented time.'

Who are these creatures and why do they treat me with such familiarity? I don't understand. It's as if they knew me. They aren't judgemental per se, but they sure think they're clever; they mock and tease me. I don't want to have anything to do with them, not yet. I can't shake the thought that I must have really fucked myself up if I'm hallucinating like this. Maybe I actually did kill myself this time. Although it's also hard to deny that if I'm still experiencing memories and hallucinations, if I'm still here at all, I must have screwed up the dose again.

I'm floating in the waters between life and death. Now I know what someone who gets hit by a bus or touches a high-tension cable must go through. There's no pain or fear. You just see yourself transported before something so enormous and astonishing that you instantly realise you're dead, and that sublime, terrifying presence can only be the beginning and the end of all things. You understand that time is a toy created to foster a sense of stability for naïve animals like me. And now that you're exiting the material realm, all times are conjugated here, in the place you're coming to. All I have to do is let myself go. But when I try, the presences return, insistent on tormenting me, holding me back.

Then Kid appears in my visions. He always does that right about now, and it's only then that I speak to him, because I can't feel any pain. I always apologise when I see him, because I feel like he could never forgive me for what I did to him when he died. I ask him to understand: I'd just lost Valerie and I was in really bad shape. He was all I had left. I remember how I used to sit on the edge of the bed to cry for Val, and the dog would come over and sit right next to me, rest his head against my ribs. And I fell apart, cried and cried.

One day I went to buy some smack from a den downtown, and before I headed back home I got comfy, cooked up a dose. Then another. I don't know how three whole days went by, but that was more or less how long I spent holed up there. Eventually some junkie left the front door open and the stupid dog got out. I'd like to think that he chased after a bitch in heat, or a fucking pork chop that fell out of a frozen goods truck. I want to believe that whatever he was looking for when he bolted out of the house was worth his while. I don't like to picture him looking for me, or that he concluded I'd abandoned him, or died. He was street-smart, that dog, and more intelligent than most humans I know. Cars never caught him off guard like that. I think he ran right out in front of it. I think he decided, now that I'd abandoned him, that it was better to die than live at the mercy of the other undead. Because for some reason I never managed to understand, that dog loved me. He looked completely intact when I came to, like he was sleeping, like he'd wake up at any moment. And I just couldn't handle it.

Yeah, I did shed a few tears at the time, but I cooked up a fix right away and shot the sadness right out of me, sprawled out next to his cold body. I knew I had to bury him, had to let him go, but I couldn't. I'd already lost everything I had, so I just kept shooting up. Since there was no garden at my place, just a little cement-paved courtyard, I brought him up to the roof and left him there so he wouldn't stink up the house. I decided I'd bury him as soon as I found a decent spot, some little piece of land where I could visit, but in the meantime I couldn't face it, couldn't even get up. I had to let myself go to shit for a while before I could say a real goodbye.

After a few days, the neighbours complained about the smell and even called the police, the assholes. They thought I was the one who'd died. By the time they came knocking, poor Kid was unrecognisable. Just a heap of fur with teeth, all dried-out and rotten. He'd flattened out into a rug. I had to stick him in a plastic bag and lug him outside, not knowing where I was going, what I was supposed to do with him. I ended up throwing him in a pile of trash. He was the best friend I ever had in my whole life, that Kid. That was around the time I started thinking of leaving the city, and also when I finally died for real, even though it may look like I'm still hanging on to life.

Like every other time I find myself approaching the threshold, I sense Kid close by, growling, barking for me to take him out. He licks my hand, tries to get me up. Just like back then, all I can feel is physical exhaustion. 'Hold on, Kid, give me a minute, man…' I tell him, 'just let me finish up here first, I won't be long. Just let me finish this and we'll go…'

I hear him whimpering, insisting. I want to stay here, to keep dreaming for a while, but he licks my face, bites at my clothes. He jumps up onto the bed and crushes my chest, pants by my ear. I can barely lift my arms to push him away.

'I'm going! Get off me, damn dog…'

I hear Kid whimper and move away, curling up aggrieved in a corner of the room. And there he stays, snorting for a while, and sometimes it sounds as if he's almost sighing, but less and less, as if all of him were drifting away, until I stop hearing him altogether. I forget about him for a bit, but I can't shake the feeling that I should have got up, that maybe I missed my stop, all because I ignored him.

Still lying there, I know I'm in the room at Don Tomás's place, immersed in absolute darkness and solitude – but I also know I'm not dead, because I can still hear the chaos in my mind. All I need to do is lift my right arm and press down on the piston of the syringe so I can empty the mixture into the veins of my left. Then I'll be in the clear. It won't be easy, but here, knocked out in my little cot, I'm in my element. I'm submerged in a conscious process of self-extinction, like a monk who sinks into the deepest meditative state and stops his heart entirely before he mummifies each cell in his body, one at a time. I've got the same austere clothes, the same protruding bones, the same ironclad will. I focus every atom of my being, and as I slowly raise my hand and make my way across the seemingly infinite stretch of nothingness above my chest before I can graze the syringe with my thumb, a gaunt and mournful woman approaches me. She strokes my hair and says she's my mother. I grope for the rough plastic of the needle, ready to inject the final drops of the concoction, but I find nothing.

I tried to wake myself up, but I felt like someone was

72

holding me down by force and shoving me into a sack. I started to think that all of this might just be another one of my opium dreams. I could still feel them jostling me around, hauling me from one place to another. I tried to resist, but I was too far gone to put up much of a fight. I heard them telling me not to struggle, not to resist, that I should just let myself be carried off to the other side. Then I did, and went still, and couldn't feel a thing.

I thought these were just visions I was having in my cot at Don Tomás's hovel. But as soon as the rush was over, I realised they weren't visions at all. Someone really had stuck me in a sack, and they really were carrying me somewhere. I think it was Don Tomás and some helper of his, and I thought I could hear the voice of Rutilo Villegas as well. Through my dream-haze, I tried to peek through the sack, and I glimpsed the silhouettes of those ragged boys peering out from the underbrush, following the entourage. I think they all thought I was dead, although maybe it was just my time in town was up and my money too and they were kicking me out at last. Now they were going to dump me in the street, high as a kite. It wouldn't be the first time it's happened to me.

I put up my best fight from inside the sack, but the last thing you want to do is fight under those conditions. You want to let the lady lead you away. She numbs you and lulls you and paralyses all your muscles, your limbs, your force of will. It was like trying to strong-arm a cotton candy. I heard them whisper that I wasn't ready, that I had to go back and take care of my unfinished business. 'Yes, yes, please, take me back, for the love of God!' I pleaded, but they didn't listen. They carried on their way and all I could do was fall back into that deep, death-like sleep. Then they dropped me onto the ground, and I lay there without moving a muscle for a long time, until I started hearing voices at close range.

10

When I opened my eyes, I found myself in a cemetery. Which made sense, in a way. Where else would they have been able to dump me? I was going to end up here sooner or later. They left me in the shade of a tree, beside a half-dug hole. I guess they'd gone behind Rutilo Villegas' back and decided to bury me in town after all. I couldn't say how long I'd been there, but I wasn't wild about the idea of going anywhere else. It was still the magic hour. It was possible that just a few minutes or hours had passed since the last rush — although it was also possible that I'd spent an entire day sprawled on the ground. Maybe that pale bluish light was no longer the glow of yesterday's dusk, but of tomorrow's dawn. Not that it mattered now.

I felt my balls and made sure I still had the tin with the kit in my underwear. They'd even tossed my stupid notebook and pencil right next to me. I leaned back, stretched out, considered my luck. Now that I had a perfect view of the sky at that hazy, crepuscular hour, and of the jungle like a wall marking the outer edge of the graveyard, now that I was in the ideal place and had all the time in the world ahead of me, there was just one problem. My tool, my fucking lucky syringe: nowhere in sight. I know there was still a single dose in there, the final decent dose, just enough to get me across the border, but I can't find it now.

All of this was a ploy to get me out of my room and steal my drugs. They think that's how they'll get rid of me, that's how they'll bump me off – and they may succeed in the end. What they don't understand is that everything will go much faster if they leave me in peace. Now I have to get back to the room, confront them, and hunt down my syringe. But I've lost my strength. I haven't been able to move an inch from here, and I'm afraid I'll collapse on my way back. I've been writing here on the ground for a while, and the shakes are lurking right around the corner. Then I'll be in serious trouble.

Maybe it's time to jump off a cliff. Now I don't even have eight pesos to buy a bullet and shoot it through my skull, supposing someone would loan me a gun. All I've got left in this life is the tin and the kit, which means a dirty syringe, the spoon, and six sad cigarettes inside. I don't even know where the cigarettes came from. There's almost no lady left. I've been scraping at it because it's my last chance to do myself in, but it's just residue at this point. I carry the tin around because if I don't I'll go crazy, and I carry the notebook because if I don't I'll be all alone. That would scare me for real.

I tried to make my way back. My body was still all stiff and numb from my lady's embrace, and I struggled to move, put one foot in front of the other. I walked the whole endless road like a corpse just emerged from its grave, passing the cemetery gate and the church, then continuing on a dirt path through lots of houses with shut doors and dark windows. When I finally made it, I found the room locked. Don Tomás had already set up the maid there. I banged on the door of his own house, but no one deigned to open up, no one ever opens up in this town; they'd sooner see you die in the street. I no longer needed a place to stay for a long stretch of time, I didn't even need a bed, just a spot to shelter in for a little while, to lie down on the concrete floor and finish what I'd started. So I smashed the glass panel in the door, unlatched it and went in. Don Tomás's maid wasn't there, she must have left for work, and all I could think is that I'd be way ahead of everyone by the time she came back.

I searched for my fix like a man possessed. I couldn't possibly have left it just lying around. I checked the drawers, behind the bed, and among the new tenant's belongings, and when I couldn't find it I figured I'd never see it again. I sat down cross-legged against the wall, ready to cook up my final jab with the syringe I had left. It was dirtier and rustier than the other one, but who cared. I got to work in a corner of the room I knew well, the one where Mike had taken out the brick that led down to the basement in those early days after I came to town. I couldn't find the loose one, though; there must be some kind of trick to it. In that moment, this decrepit corner felt like the warmest, most welcoming place I could possibly find in all of El Zapotal.

I took out the kit and started scraping off the lingering residue of smack from that sad little bag, plus the opium dust accumulated at the bottom of the tin, and started lumping it all together, every granule. I lumped and lumped everything I could from that delicate powder, and even so I couldn't gather enough for one last measly fix. So I started to sweep the film of dust off the floor and the walls, and to add the little bits of grime staining my fingers to the mix I was about to pump into my veins. I imagined that even if the dope didn't finish me off, the other filth surely would.

I didn't think I was taking too long, but I must have, because soon enough the maid turned up. She didn't like the mess I'd made, but after standing for a bit in the doorway and staring with disgust, she resigned herself and started to clean. She picked up the clothes I'd scattered all over the floor, shut the dresser drawers, and pushed the bed back into place. I guessed she'd made an agreement with Don Tomás to share the room with me for a few days, because she didn't seem surprised to find me there.

'Tomás said you don't want to leave. You stink so much I feel sick. Don't come any closer, and don't you even think of laying a hand on me or I'll have them kick you out.'

That's what she said, and then she ignored me, just like everyone else. I felt very small in that corner, making no noise, watching her potter about until she went to sleep, unsettled by my presence. I still hadn't collected enough of the stuff to cook up a proper shot. Something always interrupted me. Sometimes it was the terrified screams of the poor woman, who had night terrors and kept sitting up in bed, staring at me and asking me to leave. I told her yes, just a little longer, I was about to go. I tried to prepare my fix, but the dose kept disintegrating, maybe because of the wind or my own breath; I watched it spill again and again into the tin and onto the floor, and then I'd have to scoop it all up once more. There was less and less of that red sugar and more and more dust, more and more dirt and grit, but I was determined to shoot myself up with something, I was sure of that much. I think the woman eventually complained to Don Tomás, because first she left the room, and just when I finally felt like I'd got my space back, when I'd managed to collect the remnants and cook and get the needle ready, resting against my arm, I heard someone approach and knock on the door, slowly at first, then faster and louder.

I'm telling you, life throws you curve balls until the very end. I hesitated, wondering whether to just shoot up already and forget about everything that would happen next, or if I should go and open the door and deal with what the world was sending my way. It had to be something supremely important if it was announcing itself right at that moment, the moment when everything had come together for the grand finale. I remember thinking, *This better be important, it better not be Don Tomás wanting more money, or some other fucking ghost coming to give me hell.* But then if you don't open up, they'll come in anyway and see you wiped out on the floor and won't let you die in peace. So you have to open up, really.

I stood. I had no clothes on, but I didn't know when I lost them or they came apart. My legs quaked as if I were a newborn deer, they could barely keep me upright, and I stumbled as I made my way to the door across what felt like an infinite expanse. I opened the door and there was Rutilo Villegas, at my service, accompanied by Don Tomás, keys in hand. Don Tomás blanched at the sight of me buck naked and backed away.

'Now what do you want?' I asked Rutilo. 'You some kind of Jehovah's Witness or what? Are you here to tell me about the good news?'

Rutilo laughed gamely and didn't answer right away.

'No sir, but thanks a lot,' I continued. 'We don't believe in God in this house.'

He caught the door before I could slam it in his face.

'God doesn't give a shit about that,' he said. 'May I come in?'

I snorted, then mocked him a little to buy some time. 'Are you a cop? If you've come to arrest me, why don't you be a sport and give me ten minutes to get ready.'

'Oh come on now,' he said. 'I'm not going to lock

you up. I'm going to help you find your way out of here. We'll help you with anything you need.'

I gave him a long, hard look. He had the haughty air of all believers, like priests and missionaries. He clearly thought he was undertaking some kind of divine labour, a noble mission. At the same time, I'd always been convinced that this fucker was a cop. Not to be trusted. He had the deferential bearing of an officer who wasn't acting alone, but had been sent – and not by a person, but by a whole town that had been complaining for days, demanding he deal with the matter at hand, take the rubbish out, run off the foul junkie whose mere presence torments everyone around. And in spite of all that, there was something in his eyes that didn't seem to want to screw me over, that wanted to help. I hadn't trusted those looks for a long time.

'Is that so?' I taunted him, 'You know a doctor? Because a doctor's what I need. I'm sick and I need a prescription…'

'I'm not a doctor, but I can help you get some relief,' he said. 'Everyone knows you want to be reunited with your woman. I can help you do that. Let me in. It's for your own good.'

Well, that got me to put my trousers on and let him step into the room – not because I really thought he could lend me a hand or anything of the sort, but because, in my experience, these crooked small-town cops always know where to get some lady. Maybe trying to scrounge it up has already become a habit, an automatic move, something I do without thinking, unconscious as breathing. I bet I'll keep doing it until the day I finally die.

'Were you sent from Antonio Sierra's farm?' I pressed, but the guy didn't answer or seem interested in what I was saying. 'Maybe they gave you what they owe me. Or did you come to scare off the lost souls who are always coming to see me? I'd really appreciate that. You know this town is kind of haunted, right?'

Rutilo wandered the room, paying me no mind. Now that I'd let him in, I was alarmed by his presence: he obviously hadn't come to chat and didn't believe a word of what I'd said, and I was sure he took me for a madman. Suddenly I was worried that the town, spurred by virtue and charity in the face of my wretched condition, had paid him to shut me away and subject me to some kind of DIY rehab treatment: some deadly cocktail of tropical home remedies that would do me in after several days of abject torture.

'They owe you something from Don Antonio's farm?' he finally said. 'Well that's not good. I'll have a word with his wife.'

I finished the cigarette and tossed the butt to the ground. 'Are you really here to help me?' I asked. 'Because if you are – '

'Of course I am,' he cut me off. 'Everyone is very concerned about you, young man. They don't want you to stick around town any longer than you need to, that's all.'

I laughed in his face. 'Oh, in this hospitable little place? How kind of you. Don't you worry, mister. Like I said before, I won't be around much longer.'

Rutilo didn't react, didn't seem to mind me criticising his town. He just looked me in the eye and said, 'I'll go speak to Señora Sierra and bring back what's owed to you. But if I do that, will you promise to leave this place – and leave us in peace?'

Maybe the locals were more decent than I'd thought.

'All right,' I said. 'Bring it to me and then we'll talk.'

As soon as I'd finished my sentence, Rutilo turned and left the room. I couldn't believe it. It had been years since a normal person had done me a favour, much less got me some money with the full knowledge that I was just going to shoot it into my veins. It must have been very important to run me out of town. There was still a chance that the woman would deny the whole thing and turn the place against me – that Rutilo would come back, and not alone this time, but with Sierra's widow and a dozen farmers, people with sticks, bricks, machetes, and a couple of drums of petrol, having concluded that the best tactic was to smoke me out of my hole.

I don't know how long Rutilo was gone. I waited for him like a little kid waits for a present he's been promised. I drifted around the room, fascinated by the numbness that had overtaken my legs, as if they didn't exist, even though I could see and move them. After a while, Rutilo returned and laid the silver charms on the dresser, each set with an uncut emerald the size of a pea.

'Promise kept,' he said. 'But now we've bought the promise that you'll leave this place. We don't want to have you panting all over town, or screaming in your sleep, or dragging your feet through the streets at night. You've taken advantage of our hospitality for long enough, don't you think? We're asking nicely.'

And to think that a guy would actually pick their town to die in. They should take it as a compliment.

'Where exactly would you like me to go?' I asked.

'Go where your kind are waiting for you. Or anywhere else. But you can't stay here any more. You're no longer welcome.'

The charms were far more valuable than I'd thought. Back in the city I could have bought a ton of drugs with them. I was overwhelmed by a sense of unreality, as if everything that had happened to me since I started seeing dead people could only be the product of a fever dream. I even wondered if Rutilo Villegas himself might be one of them, and if he and those emerald charms and

82

all the rest were just a drawn-out hallucination before the lights went out in me.

'Hey,' I said, cupping the jewels like solid light in my hands, 'do you have any idea where I can make a date with the lady in this town?'

The cop seemed to know exactly what I was talking about.

'Oof,' he said. 'That's not an easy thing you're asking. Very difficult to get a date around here. There aren't many appointments, and there's so much demand. You ought to forget about all that. Take what's yours and get going. You'll never find what you're looking for here.'

'There must be someone who can help me,' I urged, begging now.

He saw the sickness in my face and softened a little. 'Try El Rincón de Juan,' he said. 'They'll help you there.'

I heard him, looked at him, thought it over. I wondered if the guy was real. It sounded like something my mind would say to keep me going, although at this point it was also entirely possible that they really were kicking me out, plain and simple. I'd worn out my welcome, spent all my money, and run out of H; now all I had left were a couple of silver and emerald charms. Maybe it was worth a try. People say Juan is the devil himself. And the devil must have a stash of smack buried in a drawer, I'm sure of it. Who knows if the earrings will be enough for him – or what he'll want in return.

11

I didn't have much to gather up when I left the room at Don Tomás's place. I left with the kit stuffed into my raggedy clothes, under the reproachful stare of Saint Villegas, who warned me that he'd take swift and decisive measures if he ever laid eyes on me again. And then it finally happened: I took the step. I've become a drifter, a vagrant with no roof over his head, no place to go. I'm not even hungry as I skulk around the streets. I can't feel my feet, as if I were floating several centimetres above the ground, travelling through the air without noticing or thinking about it or even trying to. If I find some hovel or sewer to hole up in, I'm sure I'll end up perishing of malnutrition sooner or later, maybe even before the sickness hits. But I don't want to go out like that. I want to feel the kick one last time.

Desperate now, I sat down beside a little stream and shot myself up with the residual fix I'd managed to scrape together. It wasn't much, but I need something, even a homeopathic dose or some shitty placebo, whatever. I cooked it with water from the stream, which didn't look like a drain pipe or anything, at least not at first glance. It was a really faint dose, the water was clear, barely tinted, and I didn't even feel the kick, although it must have helped at least a little. I felt slightly more lucid, but it lasted for just an instant. Now I feel awful all over again.

I'm wandering in search of El Rincón de Juan, my last chance at finding a friend, someone to save me from this torture. Maybe Beto and Rubí, or Chachi — maybe they'll remember me and lend me a hand. The chances that one of them knows where to get some lady — and feels generous enough to leave for the nearest city, run the errand on my behalf, and score me a couple of grams on credit — are null, but it's worth a try. But I never find the bar, no matter how many circles I turn. I walk past the same spots as always, and it's not like there are so many of them in this town. I pass the church again and again, the graveyard, the same houses scattered over the landscape. It's as if El Rincón de Juan had been nothing but a mirage. It starts to feel insane to even imagine that a cantina had ever existed here. My body starts to stiffen up, as if atrophying while I'm still alive, moving with a will of its own, and all I can do is follow it out of inertia.

I've been sleeping outdoors for days, like an alcoholic. At least the villagers are used to that kind of thing and don't bother you. I all but collapse with exhaustion, my knees go soft, and I'm overcome by a sleepiness so sudden and profound that I feel like I'm passing over onto the other side. I don't even have time to choose a pretty place, some spot that would make me think, 'Here, yeah, this would be a nice place for them to find me' – I just keel over wherever I am when my legs buckle and conk right out, and then it occurs to me that maybe this is it, I finally took the leap. But much to my surprise and frustration, I always open my eyes again.

Anyway, who knows how long has passed, maybe entire days. I'm losing all sense of time. The sky has been overcast for a while, and when the town isn't sunk deep in its country dark, the light seeping through the grey clouds has that vague silvery bluish colour between day and night. Something about this dusky weather agitates the insects; the town is humming with them. Everywhere I look, I see clouds of flies buzzing around the ivy, spiders perched on blades of grass, lurking in every little cavity in the soil, entrenched in the corners of the walls. When I wake up I brush off the clay dust, inescapable in this place, plus the five or six spiders that scaled my body during the night. I feel worms everywhere, in my guts, on my skin, in my brain. I can see them swimming through the watery jelly in my eyes. I knew this would happen. I know the worms aren't real, it's just the heroin fermenting my brain. But I do believe the flies and spiders are real, and that there's something about my bearing or my walking-roadkill stench that lures them to me.

There are also scorpions, lots of them. Gleaming black ones, long as my foot, and also little yellow ones, so pale that they look like albino spider babies. It's as if they've reproduced by the hundreds and emerged from the rotten wood, from under the rocks, from construction debris. They're hardy as tanks and aren't scared of people. When you cross their path, they raise their stingers and brandish them threateningly, waiting for you to get out of the way. I'm glad of this strange plague because it's the only thing that has helped me get the shakes under control. The best ones are black with red legs: a little sting from one of those and you start to feel better right away, your ears start to buzz, but after a while you have to go hunting for another, and so on and so forth every two, three hours. Soon not even that will do me any good. In eight or twelve hours, tops, it's going to hit me in a serious way; I might even be capable of killing someone for a little lady. I can feel it coming on, my blood's boiling in its pipes, throbbing in my temples, a cold sweat thickening on the skin of my face, that unsettling burn that starts to consume me. I'm waiting for the spasm of pain, which terrifies me long before it strikes, so fierce that I can only compare it to the raw pleasure I get from heroin.

There can't be more than thirty houses in the whole town, and I've banged on every single door. I've peered into the windows, which are often strangely positioned: looking onto bathrooms, or corridor walls, or the master bedroom. Many of these houses appear uninhabited – perfectly orderly and clean, but without a soul in sight besides a cat or parrot. I saw people in a few of them, but they just ignored me, no matter how hard I hammered on the doors and windowpanes. They didn't want to have anything to do with the repulsive junkie. I yelled and yelled with all my strength, as if someone were trying to murder me, screamed 'Fire!' and 'Dead! Dead! There's a fucking dead guy out here!' But no one turned on the lights in their house or came to the window. There wasn't even a cop around to take pity on me, not even a goddamned priest. It's like they're all hiding on purpose. They must be cracking up in there, entertained by the sight of me losing my mind.

A white-haired old woman wrapped in a shawl approached and spoke to me. 'You're making such a racket, young man. Can't you see we keep nice and quiet around here? Lower your voice or Rutilo will be cross, and then that's everyone's problem.'

'Hey, listen,' I blurted, doubling over, 'Where's El Rincón de Juan?'

She thought for a moment, her face creasing with confusion. 'As far as I know, there's nowhere around here with that name.'

It was no surprise that an old lady didn't know the village brothel.

'You look ill,' she told me. 'You should get some rest.'

'I need someone to help me…'

'Who doesn't, young man. Why don't you say a prayer to God, who can always spare some mercy for his children?'

And she stood there, talking to herself. I didn't know what to say to make her leave. It seems to be all they do all day: talk to themselves.

'I have faith in Our Lord Jesus Christ,' she said. 'I'm not moving an inch until He comes for me in person. I've been waiting for a long time now, but I have faith in Him. He's going to raise my body from the grave, and if have to wait until Judgement Day, when the dead are resurrected, then so be it. You'll see, Jesus Christ is coming to get me. That's what he promised in His Gospel…'

She kept on murmuring like this as she drifted away. I don't know why I feel like the devil's going to be more helpful this time. I have to find El Rincón de Juan. I need to scream and slap him around, need to shake him and beg, throw a crazy tantrum and threaten to haunt him in his dreams and doom him to a dead man's curse if he doesn't help me. If he won't budge even then, well, I'll just burn the place down. I have nowhere else to go. I swear that if I find my syringe, even if it's buried in a pile of muck at the bottom of a landfill, I'll give thanks to God and shoot up right then and there. And if I never find it, then I'll die terrified, hallucinating skeletons and snakes, struck down by the crippling shock that will stop my poor heart.

You forget this sense of urgency no matter how well you know it. When the sickness hits, everything's backwards. If you're cold, it feels like your blood is boiling; if you're hot, your veins freeze inside you. When you're exhausted you can't sleep, and if you're awake you're overpowered by a fatigue so fierce it's like swimming in molasses. You can go for days without food, and when your appetite finally stirs and you try to eat, your stomach is out of service. Impossible to push anything other than yogurt down there. Breathing, vomiting, light: everything is pain, and all you want is to get rid of it.

It's the most overwhelming sensation on earth. Like an itch. Your brain is programmed to force the body to scratch itself, or else a hungry leopard will tear you to pieces. There you are, all keyed up, running this way and that, sweating, crying, but there's nothing chasing you at all. Your body gradually shuts itself off, and there comes a moment when it's only fuelled by withdrawal: the inner alarm that blares when you don't shoot up and makes your mind think you're going to die. Any effort to deactivate it is futile. The only thing that can muffle it for a while is another dose of H.

12

When I'm not slumped in some ditch to sleep or write in my notebook, I wander the streets in my on-going funeral march, trying to stave off the sickness. I call them funeral marches because they're deathly depressing, and because they always end in burials, yours or someone else's. They bring back lots of memories. After all, I've spent much of my life this way. Scoring heroin is the closest I've had to a job since I was a teenager, and I've got pretty good at it. This hadn't happened to me for a long time, but even the best fisherman will starve to death in the desert.

I've spent years devoted to the rush. That's why I'm all atrophied and skinny and covered in sores. It's like spending your whole life staring straight at the sun, or travelling at the speed of light. My memories of the past decade are warped by a buzzing in the background. They're fragmentary, because most of those years have been one long, all-encompassing, nearly continuous opium dream. I don't know if it's the shakes or some kind of terminal hallucination, but as I drift around I find myself remembering parts of what my life used to be, and I feel the need to stop and really register them, because soon they'll slip away again through the cracks of my mind, all gnawed-at and corroded by drugs.

I remember when Valerie got hooked, when she started liking the lady too. We'd go fishing together, equally sick, equally scared, but I knew the drill already. I'd spent years doing the same thing with Mike and Elisa and Romuel. We knew that if you're going to make it in the business, you'd better bend the rules, and the rules themselves lose all meaning when your objective is so clear. It was sweet, actually, because Valerie would start to worry and I'd calm her down, promise her we'd figure it out, everything would be fine, and I taught her how and took care of her and in the end we always came through. You should've seen the way Val looked at me afterwards, with those huge, admiring almond-shaped eyes of hers, as if I were the best, the most bad-ass man of all men walking the earth. Some people live a hundred years without ever feeling anything like that, but I did. I did feel it.

Everything's easier with a girl by your side, and my Valerie learned the ropes right away. She'd always been so refined, so well-mannered, but she turned out to be the biggest delinquent of the lot. She had a genuine talent for conning people. Which I knew already, because that's what she did to me: she hooked me and never let me go. I think that's how we spent the happiest moments of our relationship, out and about, our arms around each other, jonesing a little, with a white light glancing off the wet asphalt, sharing cigarettes, waiting under the awning of some shuttered store for the rain to pass so we could step out and wander the neighbourhood again. We mostly just slept the rest of the time, or fucked, or fought. Impossible to predict that you'd eventually remember such shitty days as the best of your life, but yeah, that's what happens.

Normal people can't imagine holding up a pharmacy with your friends as if you were invading a military barracks in the name of revolution, can't imagine confronting a cop who's aiming a gun at you because fear doesn't exist any more, can't imagine having the power to make money materialise out of thin air, because you don't really need it. I'd stop strangers in the street, tell them I was sick and needed medicine, and they'd fork over their cash at the sight of me. We never had to resort to guns or knives, because there's no sight more alarming than a resuscitated corpse coming up to you unprovoked and begging for medication money. As if there were anything in the world that could have cured our sickness back then.

In any case, people spend their money poorly. We were doing them a favour by taking it off their hands. We made better use of it, because we didn't even need the cash; it never mattered to us, it wasn't what we wanted. It was just a means to an end. If people knew what H was, they wouldn't want money any more. Maybe smack itself would be money. A piece of paper, even a gold nugget – what the hell does that do for anybody? This shit, though, is the portal to paradise. You can pinch anything else in life when no one's watching, or get it for free if you have friends. Even though you turn into a disgusting junkie and nobody invites you over any more, even though it gets harder to go unnoticed in your average dive, you get better and better at it, evolving to make it through. Like it or not, you adapt. It's what we've got in common with cockroaches.

You do end up stealing a lot, costing society a pretty penny. You'll be surprised at what can fit in your underwear, your armpits, every nook and cranny of your body. Lord knows how I stayed out of jail all those years, but one thing I'm sure of is that a prison stint would have been an all-inclusive holiday for me. I've heard people say that the only time in their lives they managed to clean out their pipes was in the clink. Which doesn't make sense to me, because people also say you can work for smack in prison.

Once I even thought of trying to get myself locked up. I was so tired, felt like I needed a hospital or an insane asylum, or why not, a jail, a roof over my head, someplace where they'd give me food and blankets and I could see a doctor. So I went up to a couple of cops and handed over my kit. But the fucking pigs treated me like a dog – they tossed it onto the ground and laughed in my face. I didn't interest them because they weren't going to squeeze any cash out of me. They said throwing me in the can was going to cost the state more than they wanted to spend. That they were better off if I just kept shoplifting while I hurried up and died. Please, I said, do me a favour, I just needed a little break. Otherwise I'd end up stabbing someone, and of course I didn't want to resort to that, did I. Well then I'd just have to figure it out myself, good luck getting some rest. That's what they told me.

It's not like nobody tried to help. My dad did his best to get me out of there, but he never really embraced me, not like my lady did. I'd slip out and vanish for weeks at a time, and if he tracked me down or I returned home much later, once everyone had taken me for dead, the thing that made it home was less and less 'me' all the time. It was some other animal that emerged as if from underground, crawling out of some hollow dense with filth and blood and rats. It gets harder and harder to come back, and when you do it's practically a miracle, something that shouldn't even have happened. People see you as a total freak, someone who isn't supposed to be there, who should be dead, or who was dead and came back to life.

Regaining sensation after all that numbness is sheer torture, a process you never fully recover from. I went through it several times. But I've had my fill, I'm not doing that again. It would kill me, and besides, I know there's nothing to come back to. Life is like a kind of refrigerator: time has an effect on things and anything of value is like a carton of milk, souring and breaking down while you're unplugged, plunged into darkness. When you're back, once you're cured, you feel like you're missing something of great importance, like an arm or an eye, doomed to hobbling through life on crutches.

When my old man died and I collected my inheritance, there was nothing else to get in the way of my plan. I don't want to think I killed him, but it can't have been easy on the guy. Sometimes I can't help but think that when his heart finally gave out it was because of how hard he'd tried to keep up with me. I wonder what it was like to see his son turn into this, a seedling that had sprouted and grown in the depths of a cave, blind, albino, maybe a little monstrous, a mutant not fit to be seen, meant to lurk in the shadows. He always tried to save me and I'm grateful now, no matter how useless it was. He couldn't understand that I belonged underground, or maybe he just didn't know how to love me like that, the way I was. There aren't many places in this world where people can grasp the existence of beings like me, the undead who've been buried and dug up again so many times that they no longer participate in society and have been permanently cast off by it. When they do, they call us zombies.

I felt profoundly alone when I started letting my friends into the house my dad left me. I liked it at first because we'd shoot up together and there was always enough to go around. It was comforting to see my friends' faces all around me, and when the flash overtook me, the place felt a little like all the drug dens I've ever been to: like a lavish palace trimmed with gold and purple ornaments, exquisitely refined, full of warmth and affection, kind and familiar eyes.

Word spread fast that the doors were open at my house, that there were couches and a sofa, that the dealer came by twice a day. It quickly devolved into something like a graveyard, a zombie settlement. I always kept my room blocked off from all that, but when I'd get up high for a glass of water, I'd find them scattered all over the house. You had to walk on tiptoe, treading carefully to keep from stepping on them. There was trash and syringes everywhere you looked, and the house smelled like rank bodies and stale smoke. That was the sumptuous palace I ended up spending those last months in.

Later, when you stir from your stupor and search the crowd for your friends, it gets harder and harder to find them. You unearth them all contorted behind a couch, packed into the bathtub. More and more often, those familiar faces turn into stiff, ashen, thin-lipped objects you end up dropping off in front of the hospital. One day you wake from a particularly generous rush, and when you start to shift and prod at the heaps of corpses, you don't recognise a single face. You realise that all your friends have gone, and you've spent days, maybe weeks, in the company of strangers who only came to shoot up heroin in your living room, because what used to be your home has become the most popular trap house in the north of the city.

I always thought I liked that house because I grew up there. I have lots of memories in that place, some good, many from when it was just me and my dad. I remember cloudy evenings that smelled like whiskey, tobacco and orange blossoms, I remember him dancing to the jazz that drifted up through the murmur of the rain, watching old science fiction movies on TV. But the house, and the childhood memories peeking out through my dreams when I lived there, was also deeply unsettling to me. Looking back on it, I think it was because the old man stuck around for years after he died. There he was, on and off but for a good long while, standing in the doorway, clutching his chest and begging me to change, be a good boy, do something constructive with my life. Just like when he was alive. I don't think he ever stopped worrying. It unnerves me to think that maybe he did care about me after all, much more than he ever deigned to admit. I couldn't grasp it before, but I think that's part of why I ran away from home. All I felt was loneliness there, and hearing my dad's voice all day long was just too much. There's no solace or companionship in the voices of the dead. All you hear is their absence.

I think what you end up trying to cure yourself of, deep down, is the loneliness you feel whenever the rush is over, when you realise you're ending up all alone, your friends are dying one by one, and those who don't die are leaving, abandoning you. Just like my family abandoned me for selling my soul and turning to scum, just like my mother abandoned me in the very act of giving me life. So did my Valerie, even, by wanting to catch up with me. The only one who never abandons you is the lady. She's always willing to welcome you back, and only she will ever give you something like that, something like love, an embrace so tight that sometimes you can hardly breathe. You wind up like me, leaving everything behind, fleeing the city because there's nothing worse than being surrounded by people and still feeling alone. But just look where you end up. The most godforsaken town in the world.

13

I've been lying in this ditch on the side of the road for hours, and I haven't stopped writing because it's the only thing that can distract me. The pain pulsing in my head is so intense that I struggle to make out the letters forming on the page, and I'm tired of walking. I'm tired of always ending up at the graveyard, as if all roads in town led back to it. I don't want to go in there because I know I'll never come out if I do, and I don't want to set foot in the church because I'm not in the mood for sermons. I don't want to know what I've done wrong. All I need is a good shot to send me off to the other side. Maybe if I keep writing here I won't even notice when I run out of juice; maybe I won't even feel the sickness hit, I'll just stop breathing. It's coming, I can feel it.

Only the dead will bother you here. They never rest. Sometimes I try to close my eyes and sleep, but I'm besieged by the voices. Once, drifting in dreams, Antonio Sierra appeared and sat down beside me. 'Hang on now, kid, don't fall asleep yet,' he said. 'Listen up, I want to return the favour…'

I was writhing around in that ditch, my stomach seizing up. Asking me to listen was like asking a patient with renal colic to spell his own name. All I could think was 'A favour, a favour. Everyone in this town wants to do you a fucking favour and guess where that gets you.'

'Are you going to tell me where my lady is?' I yelped from where I lay.

'I can't, because I still haven't found mine. I want to answer the question of yours that my wife couldn't. I want to help you rest. I want you to know that you're not crazy,' he said, 'and you're not hallucinating. We're real, us dead people, and you're becoming one of us.'

'No, no, no,' I insisted. 'Not me, I'm not going to be some debt-haunted spectre, I'm going to find peace on the other side, I've seen it, I know it well… it's only because of the goddamn shakes that I can see you now, but it'll pass, you'll see, and then I'll get out of here and be reunited with my lady…'

'No one can get out of here. At most, you'll find your way to El Rincón de Juan, but I don't think the Señora will let you in. It's worth a try, though.'

This is the kind of trick my body plays on me. That's how it gets me up out of this sewer and back on my own two feet. When I tried to question Antonio Sierra, he had already gone, and I just clutched my belly and waited for the cramps to ease so I could keep going.

I have no choice but to drag myself about until I find the cantina. Now I'm really descending into hell. This is what happens as the effect of the lady wanes: you start to feel things again, mostly miserable ones, and your heroin-hungry brain starts hunting for what it misses in simpler pleasures.

I ate a cigarette a little while ago. It wasn't much, but the bitter taste of the tobacco numbed my hunger some. I'm not even sure it's hunger for food, because all I can imagine eating is lady, and I feel like not even that could sate me. The cigarette gave me a boost; my belly cramp relaxed into an electrical tickle. It gave me a strange sensation of pleasure I hadn't felt in a long time. I still have a bitter taste in my mouth, but now I can move around again. It's hard to find El Rincón de Juan at this twilight hour, without the halogen bulb to serve as a beacon in the darkness. The village is sunk into its usual desolation; at least there are dogs. They know me and I know them. Maybe because I've spent so much time alone, I get the feeling that they can talk to me, staring at me with their inquisitive eyes: 'Hey, what's up, Bonesy? Haven't kicked the bucket yet?'

And I respond: 'Nope. How about that? Still out here, giving people hell.'

They follow me and bark when they hear rustles in the underbrush to scare off snakes and predators. I get the sense that they're scaring off people, too, letting them know I'm coming. I can hear them slam the doors and windows of their houses, and in the distance I can see them switching off the lights before I get there. Everything around me takes on a ghostly aura and doesn't revive until I'm a few blocks away.

Every once in a while a family walks by, or a shepherd with his goats, but they just quicken their step and move away. People don't scare me because I know I scare them. If I were a normal person and ran into myself, I'd be pretty freaked out too. I ask the occasional passers-by for directions, but no one knows El Rincón de Juan. It feels like they're lying – in a village so small, how can it be that no one knows what time it is, or where the cantina is, or where to find a fix? It's like they live in another era, captive to a kind of frenetic monomania. One woman weeps and holds out an infant to me – but all that's swaddled in the blankets is a river stone.

'Please,' she says, 'hold my baby.'

I act as if I don't see these people. I try to hasten my cadaverous pace and keep going. They carry on their way, too, not wasting a moment of distress.

I walk for what feels like days or weeks before I run into another one, and just as I start to approach him and ask about the bar, he flinches and draws back.

'Begone, Satan!' he shouts from a distance. 'You should be worshipping Lord Jehovah… even a dead man who believes in Him will live, and anyone who's still alive and believes in Him will never die… He has given me the power of crushing snakes and scorpions… now nothing can harm me…'

I don't know who these people are or why they tell me this stuff, or if they say the same things to everyone they run into along this road. I wonder if they might be dead, if maybe I'm just hallucinating people who are hallucinating me, and that's why no one knows anything. Or maybe they're alive and just crazy. When I pass women, they cross themselves warily. They put themselves between me and their kids when I speak to them, cover their ears. The kids go pale and hold their breath at the sight of me, and when I look back they hide behind their mother's skirts' and lift rocks from the ground, and that's how I realise I'm the creature from scary stories told by adults, the monster who hunts down disobedient children. Sometimes I look at their blanched, terrified faces and know it's actually even worse. I know what they really see in me: I'm the kid who misbehaved. I'm the moral of the story.

At the edge of the jungle, I see peasants in grubby rags, sprinting through the trees, machetes in hand, their faces wild and dark with dirt, shouting at me to run, they're coming. I don't understand who's coming, and before I can ask they vanish into the brush again. I know I can't fight or flee in my current state; anyone who wants to track me down will easily catch up with me. I'm low-hanging fruit for a lynx or a jaguar, which would only have to pounce from a tree branch for me to split in two. I must not look all that appetising, though; I bet they'd prefer something meatier and less toxic. So I don't worry much. The dogs guide me along, leading me where I need to go.

My mind is stamped with the thought of my syringe and its half-dose. I can see it right in front of me. Wherever I'm walking, that's where I'm bound. As night falls, my fix is the only thing I can make out in the dense, moonless dark. As I advance, I curse the villagers who refused to help me. If I get one last wish before I die, I swear, I'll wish for them to see my cadaverous face every night of their lives, for my body to return and torment them and suffocate them in dreams, for remorse to eat away at them until the last of their days, just as the sickness will eat away at me.

It may not be the most Christian of final sentiments, but I never was a Christian, and it seems perfectly reasonable under the circumstances. Even so, I'm willing to make a concession and put it down in writing: Lord, if You exist and help me find one last dose, I promise to go quietly, without sorrows or resentments, forgiving everyone, and then it's just a matter of You forgiving me for all the havoc I wreaked on earth. But we can negotiate that part after the rush.

14

The sky was still overcast when I woke. I'd slept by the cement wall of an abandoned construction site in the middle of a vacant lot. There was no noise or motion during the night, and this morning I don't even hear any birdsong. I feel like I've been wandering for weeks, but judging by my symptoms it can't have been more than a couple of days. I'm barely starting my descent.

I got up and stumbled around the shell of the building, which might have been a neglected storage space or a slaughterhouse, until I reached a metal door, barred with a padlock and steel chain. I looked up and found the Corona Light sign, dirty and broken, hanging under a lamp with a blown halogen bulb, and in the dim dawn light I managed to decipher the faded letters: El Rincón de Juan. But it looked shuttered, or as if it had never existed at all. There were no drunks lying around, no bottles or cigarette butts, no scraps of food or garbage. Nothing to indicate that the spot had been frequented by a single soul in many months.

Now I drift around the concrete cube, looking for some kind of gap that will give me a glimpse inside, but I can't find so much as a crack for the light to come through. There's nothing but bare ground beyond it, with piles of junk and gravel strewn about the fields. It still feels very early in the morning, but I don't see any mule drivers, no traces of smoke. No cockerels crowing, no lumber lorries scraping and groaning their way over the earth, nor the engines of chainsaws up in the hills, and I wonder if it's possible that everyone has just left town overnight. It's like the world froze on Sunday. A little like my whole life has always been. All I can do is wait for the church bells to ring and see if anybody's still out there.

The atmosphere is sheer loneliness and desolation. But the jungle gives off a magnetic hum that catches my attention, and from the slope where I find myself outside El Rincón de Juan, I can make out the haciendas in the distance. In the bluish glow of the morning, the walls once painted a dull pink have taken on a crimson, almost bloodlike hue, and stifling vines throb like the tentacles of some underground animal, preparing them to be swallowed, dragged into the depths of the earth. Despite the isolation and erosion of the walls, the haciendas are the only places in town that feel alive at that hour. Some kind of multitude jounces and shudders inside, as if the village fair were being held out there in the distance, too far for the music to reach me where I stand, but the ground trembles with an echo that courses through kilometres of low, dense, impenetrable jungle.

The sight of the haciendas dazzles, fascinates and unsettles me too. I feel like that's where I should be, but there's no way for me to reach them. It makes sense to stay here, even though I feel like that's where I belong. I can only compare the sensation to what I felt back in the day with Jairo, Cleto and Mike, when we'd go to parties in the woods, getting lost, searching for hours. We'd follow the *boom-boom-boom* of the speakers and drums, like a distant heartbeat, and we felt like our lives would be happening somewhere else until we found them.

We ran away from home together, and we believed that those massive raves were our real place in the world, where we knew we'd find the faces of all our long-lost friends in the crowd. We'd leave in search of home, but we were already lost boys, so all we did was get even more lost. That's what always happened to us. Sometimes we couldn't find the party at all, so we'd stop somewhere in the woods and put on our own music, pull out the powder, time to dance, time to lose ourselves in the drugs, in that wild sensory cascade. And we started to find our people there, little by little; started to find what we gradually called our 'home'. And the lady, well, the lady is the lady of the house, the great matriarch. She wasted no time in taking the reins.

I don't think many of us returned to our actual homes after that. It was hard to go back, especially because by that point we were all somehow foreigners in our own lives. Normal people cling to stuff. Ever since I was very small, I understood that things will leave you of their own accord, so I clung to nothing. Only to H. By comparison, I don't think that's bad at all. It's almost like being a monk, except you're clinging to something that actually exists.

I think about all this with my eyes fixed on the distant, imposing walls of the haciendas. It's like time hasn't passed at all, like the town is still sunk in a kind of limbo, a static stupor. All that diverts my attention from the ephemeral daydream cast onto the dome of my skull is a rhythmic, metallic sound, like an animal struggling with the padlock to the door. I hurry to circle the structure so I can figure out what other presence is there, besides me, in this landscape as desolate and motionless as the aftermath of a nuclear disaster. It wouldn't surprise me to find a monster, some mutant with deformities that keep it from interacting with other creatures, or a terrible predator devouring everything in its path. Those are the presences it would make sense to find here, lost with me at the edge of the world.

Before I reach the entrance, I hear a fierce, melancholy whistle intoning a mischievous song. It's like there are multiple voices sounding that single trill, conjugating notes as if they were almost simultaneous, like an accordion. When I get to the front I see a young man with coppery skin, long black shoulder-length hair and a goatee. He's dressed in black, and even though his clothes aren't especially elegant, he has a refined air about him. He doesn't seem to notice me at first and keeps working clumsily to open the padlock.

'Are you Juan?' I ask.

Without startling or otherwise reacting to my presence, the guy continues to wrangle with the chain. All he does is give me the once-over. 'So you made it. Welcome.'

Then he looks back down and keeps trying each of an enormous handful of keys, more keys than all the doors that could possibly exist in El Zapotal.

'Do you know who I am?' I ask.

'How couldn't I know. The whole town knows who you are. You're the latest Bonesy. How can I help you?'

He's familiar to me somehow. As he wrestles with the door, I start to drag my way over to him, trying to remember where I'd seen his face before.

'I was wondering if you had a little horse I could buy.'

The guy nods absentmindedly. Not even looking up, he answers as if I'd asked him the most normal question in the world. 'A horse costs a couple of thousand, but you can have a goat for four fifty. Great meat.'

'Wait, no', I say, mimicking the gesture of shooting up. 'You know what I mean... material, right? For a date with the lady.'

He lifts his head and takes a long look at me, smiling, curious. 'You want to make a date with the Lady?'

I can feel my nostrils clear, my eyes widen like grape-fruits. I may have even ventured a smile.

'That can be arranged,' he says, 'but you probably know that the Lady is a very jealous lover. Fickle, too.'

'Oh, sure, I definitely know...' I answer eagerly.

'And she's busy. Not easy to catch her. Can you pay?'

'Some, yeah,' I say, extracting the charms from my pockets. 'I just need a little, really...'

He looks at the charms, then back at me, perplexed, as if I were crazy. 'What do you mean, a little? I'll get it all for you, the whole thing.'

I felt my entire body contort with anguish, a hot ripple of adrenaline.

'The whole thing? Sorry? What are you talking about?'

'The Lady, what else. The most popular whore in town. Maybe the entire world. But what are you talking about, then?'

'Uh, lady... some horse, a drop of smack for my sad old veins...'

The guy laughs in my face.

'No sir. There's none of that around here. Can you imagine what would happen if there were, considering how sad and bored people are? It'd be the death of this town.'

I look around. It's getting dark, as if night is falling, even though the day never dawned.

'Isn't the town dead already?'

'For some it is,' he replies. He stops trying to pick the lock and tosses aside the keys in frustration.

Crouching to rummage in a leather backpack, he extracts a screwdriver and a hammer and starts to bang on the lock, trying to break it. I watch and shout over the racket.

'There must be a little that someone left behind. Everyone says you're the boss around here.'

The lock clangs in a burst of white sparks with every hammer-blow.

'They say you're the devil himself.'

The guy laughs and doesn't bother to look up. 'People say all kinds of things. Some are even true.'

'What,' I try to tease, 'that's not true?'

He grins, glancing at me. But then he shakes his head, fed up, tired of explaining.

'I'm just the guy in charge.'

'In charge of what?'

'Well, for now, of trying to open this door.'

And he keeps banging and banging and it becomes impossible to even talk over all the racket. I study him and wonder if he could be a thief, just some random dude taking advantage of the town's deserted state to loot stores, houses, businesses. I wonder if he's playing along, pretending to be Juan because I asked him first. Maybe he doesn't even exist and I'm talking to myself, seeing mirages like someone lost in the desert, and my mind is playing tricks on me, reciting nonsense to keep me entertained.

'So you really can't help me?'

My knees are giving out again and I have to sit back down. The guy finally gives up and drops his tools beside the keys. He takes out a pack of cigarettes and flops down next to me.

'Well, I can make you an appointment with the Lady,' he says, holding out the pack of cigarettes. I take one with a trembling hand. 'What do you say? There's really nothing better, let me tell you. Puts an end to all your troubles. You find peace in her arms.'

'Didn't you say it's hard to get a date? I mean, just look at me, I don't think she'd be up for it.'

He strikes a match to light my cigarette, then his.

'She's usually booked, that's all. But the Lady's up for everyone. Seems to me that you're the one who's not ready. You're scared or something. Otherwise you would've gone to see her a long time ago.'

I don't know this guy from Adam and it feels like he's getting a little too confident. I bristle: 'Watch out, OK? I don't like being called a coward. That lady you're talking about, how could I be scared of her? I came here to face the stuff that terrifies everybody else. And I've always had the upper hand. So get this through your head,' I say emphatically, 'I'm not scared of anything. Not even death. Got that?'

The guy nods and gazes out into the distance, takes a drag on his cigarette. Then I hear him say with a sigh, ''Course, buddy. Of course I get it. All I'm saying is that some people do get a little scared and there's no shame in that. It makes sense. Because once you make your date with the Lady, there's no turning back. You feel like you can finally unwind, and you enter this peaceful place that some people don't want to leave. You have to give her everything you ever had in life. There's no other way.'

All of this sounds like something I'd been told before, but mostly it fills me with a sadness that makes my eyes tighten and well with tears.

'I don't have anything left. All I want is my lady. That's all I'm asking for.'

We sit there for a while, staring at the jungle on the horizon. From time to time I shift to look at him, taking in his coppery skin, shining in the glow of the dusk, or dawn, or whatever ethereal time it is. I'm not sure if he's really there. He reminds me of myself, a being who wasn't really of this world, maybe another ghost. But here he is, smoking in silence, a smile curling at the corner of his mouth.

I think about what I've heard. Yes, the lady is my greatest love, my longest relationship. Her absence has always made my stomach ache like no other longing or lack, no other lovesickness. Sitting here, I feel the H leaving my veins, and I start to recover all the sensations I'd anaesthetised for all these years. That sudden wave of chemicals bursting the dam and flooding my brain, the overwhelming rush of nostalgia and distress that sears all the way into my innards – what I've always called an illness – is maybe what others would just call being alive. It's been ages since I've felt the spasm of being alive so acutely, close as I am to death. Trembling and shuddering on the stoop, waiting for the cramps to hit, I start to understand that the feeling I've tried to avoid for so many years – this pain – is my real home, the place inhabited by everyone I left along the way.

The guy watches me sidelong, notes me twitching in silence.

'How long has it been since you last saw her, your lady?'

I think about it, but in my state it's hard to be sure. 'I don't know. How long have we been sitting here?'

The guy glances away and mutters something I can't make out. Everything feels like a dream.

'I feel really bad. I feel like I'm dying without her.'

'You know, something tells me you're already forgetting about her. I don't think you need her any more. I've got something better for you. Come on, take my offer.' Then he falls silent and smiles.

Sometimes people turn up during the worst of your jonesing and try to help you out. They coax you to this place or that, present you with the fix you'd been looking for, or talk you into getting yourself locked up and having your pipes cleaned out once and for all. I still don't know what this one is up to, but he clearly wants to take me somewhere.

'I really think you could use a date with the Lady. It'll do you good,' he says.

'And you're sure you can arrange it?'

He smiles and says with pride, almost arrogance, 'I'm the doorman. I decide who goes in and who waits outside.'

'Do you think I'll get to go in? And that she'll agree to see me? Everybody's always saying something different, so I just don't know if I'll ever meet her for real.'

'Amigo,' Juan says with a smile, 'she's the only woman in the world who needs no introduction, because everyone knows her already. And if not, they'll meet her really soon.'

I stare at him with my dry, vacant eyes.

'I can't pay, though. All I've got are these silver charms,' I explain, opening my palm. 'But I wanted to buy my H with them.'

His eyes gleam at the sight of the silver and emeralds. He plucks them from my hand and turns them over, examining them for a moment, before he loses interest and gives them back.

'These are worthless here,' he said. 'But don't you worry, everyone manages to pay their way.'

My soul is pretty worthless, too, although I wasn't about to say that. I was going to wait until he figured it out himself.

'Where do I have to go?'

Juan gestures to the jungle in the distance, to the walls of the ruined haciendas. 'Out there,' he says. 'To All-Souls' Hill.'

I study the tract of jungle between us and them and can tell it's going to be a long, arduous road. I don't say a word, but I know I won't get anywhere without my lady.

'It's a hike, but it's worth it,' he adds. 'Everything you're looking for is there. Lots of people like you who've come here, who've got lost or disappeared, they've all headed that way.'

I remember my opium dream from those first few days, the feeling that all of my dead friends were here.

'Is there a trap house?' I ask.

The guy grins and shakes his head. 'Close. A community, you might say. You'll find everything you need. And you'll certainly find the Lady.'

It sounds like a generous offer: a one-way trip to a place of rest you'll never return from. That's exactly what I'm in the market for. I don't want to admit it, but I'm nervous about the trip.

'Can't you help me?' I ask. 'Why don't you go and make sure she has the goods? I'll wait for you. I'm not going anywhere.'

'Let's do this,' he proposes. 'You go, make your own way, see if you find what you're looking for. Once you're ready, I'll send my guys to pick you up. Careful, though, or you'll end up wandering the town in search of your lady, blubbering and scribbling in that notebook of yours forever, and you'll never finish dying.'

Juan gives me a pat on my bony knee, flashes a faint smile, and gets to his feet. The metallic hammering resumes, the blows pounding in my head with unprec-edented force, like a migraine pulsing in some deep cerebral artery. How do they expect me to stop drifting around if they keep sending me every which way? Pure bureaucracy – I'm redirected from window to window in search of the certificate-request form for the approval of preliminary permission, and meanwhile I just get sicker and sicker. I feel like if I let my body regain sensation, it'll also regain the one thing I do want to avoid at all costs: the fear. The panic I feel, as if I were trapped in an airless space, suffocating to death.

I can't remember the last time I went so long without my lady. As far as I recall, this becomes a descent into a feverish, delirious inferno after just a couple of days. I should be writhing in pain by now – although I guess in a sense I already am. Why won't this hellish sickness finally run its course? It toys with me, threatens to drag me under, but it never knocks me down. Or am I already laid out in some hallucinatory ditch where none of this is really happening?

Why do I feel like I can still get up and out of here? I even sense my arms and legs getting a little stronger. Maybe it's the nicotine, or the jonesing itself, the energy channelling my bilious, atrophied body towards the fix, more powerful than I am. It lifts me a few centimetres off the ground and lets me float from place to place as I try to quell my ghostly hunger. With my guts churning like a washing machine, unable to hit pause even for an instant, barred from getting off the rollercoaster – this must be hell, and I've been living here for days now.

15

The metallic battering went silent a while ago, but I didn't even notice, because the throbbing in my head never stopped. I can't find Juan anywhere, and the door is still chained shut. He said he'd keep trying, but I think it's time for me to accept that I'll never find my lady, and I'll probably die of withdrawal on the side of the road. My body likely can't survive that, not here, not in such a state, with no one to take care of me. I can't believe I'm going out this way. That was never the plan, I never imagined I'd burn through all the smack I brought. But look at me now, a bottomless pit, devouring everything in its path, all forms, all light.

I can't stop now. It's a long journey to All-Souls' Hill, and that's where I'm headed now, more out of resignation than necessity at this point. I feel like I'm going in circles, my muscles cramping, stiffer with every turn. If someone ran into me now, they might only see a skin-sack of guts, moaning and floating over the earth, smoking – I've still got two cigarettes left. And they'd see the appearance and disappearance of electrical highways, circulatory branches, my nerves and veins, blinking and twinkling like Christmas lights, cohering as I feel and create them with my consciousness, then vanishing again as soon as I forget.

I'm regaining sensation in my whole body, and of course all my old aches and pains resurge with it. Not just the toothaches and stomachaches I've ignored for years, ulcerating into agony. I mean other hurts. The anguish of it all. When the shakes hit, the first thing I feel, and the first thing I want to soothe, is anxiety. I've felt it all my life, the panic I get when I'm alone, and I remember it eased a bit when I went to those huge parties with my friends. Maybe what calmed me down wasn't the drugs, but just having other people around, seeing my friends' faces. Drugs only meant that my friends would always be there, would always come back, would never abandon me.

Now there's no one left. At least I used to have the lady, but now I'm all alone. And since my mind believes that what I want is to see my friends, it's sending them back to me one by one, and there they are. I glimpse their bodies stripped of flesh, their heads appear before me on the path. As I pass them, they mock my funeral march, or else they try to cheer me on: 'How's the sickness treating you, bro?'

I turn and see Jairo's head perched on a boulder, and a few metres ahead, set into a chink in a rockfall, there's Romuel's. He chimes in: 'Are you kidding? My buddy here isn't just jonesing... he's going through some serious shit.'

'He's got the whole damn jungle on his back, poor dude.'

Jairo lets out a sputtering laugh. Romuel continues: 'Just look at him. My buddy here's gone cold turkey!'

'Cold turkey? Nah, man, this guy's made it to the big leagues. He's a bona fide penguin.'

The assholes are laughing at me. Even as I flee, I can hear them jeer.

'Cold as a polar bear…'

I walk on. A few steps ahead, I see Elisa floating among the trees, just a head trailing some innards. 'You got this, flaco,' she urges. 'You're almost there, you're so close. You're going to get that fix, the sweetest you've ever had.'

Beside her, emerging from the shadowy underbrush, comes her brother Christ with his heart exposed, raising his hand in a slow wave.

'Hang in there,' he says. 'The best nap in the world is waiting for you, buddy.'

I don't know if this is all a symptom of withdrawal or something else entirely. I've got the shakes so many times, and this process, no matter how hard it tries to pass itself off as just a wicked detox, no matter how hard it tries to imitate just that – this is a whole different beast. This arduous, cyclical retreat along a rocky path, overgrown with weeds, makes me feel trapped. Maybe this tortuous moment before death is what people call purgatory. Some reach it in their beds; others visit it for an instant before their hearts give out. But I've been wandering it for ages now.

The village darkens around me, the trees and their foliage blur into the background, the contours of the houses dim, as if the whole place were draining of light. Or maybe I'm going blind. I walk straight ahead without encountering a single obstacle or exiting the town limits. I still haven't found the road to All-Souls' Hill, but as I search I come across a stone cabin shining from the inside. I see five kids kneeling on the floor, holding hands, a lit candle in the middle of the circle. The oldest is a girl who looks to be about sixteen.

'What are you doing?' I call out to them, and they all flinch. Only the girl turns to look at me. The youngest of the group opens his eyes and struggles to focus his vision on me. It looks like he has an eye infection: they're red and swollen, caked with gunk. The others turn away or close their eyes anxiously, or else they sit still, pale, looking hard at each other, or at the girl, who answers me: 'We've been waiting for you.'

I don't want to scare them, so I say, 'I'm looking for my lady. Any chance you have a little to spare?'

The girl studies me as the little boy rubs his puffy eyes, trying to get a good look through the crust. Two of the kids are twins and look so much like the girl that they must be her brothers. They fix her with a steady stare, then exchange glances. A fifth teenager roves the room with his eyes, taking in the scene with restlessness, even fear. He's clearly uncomfortable with my presence. 'Come on, let's get out of here,' he pleads again and again.

The others ignore him. When he gets up to leave, the girl stops him, sits him back down. None has the guts to look at me directly except for her and the kid with the swollen eyes. She turns and pulls a dish out of a backpack, then starts to prepare something inside it. When she sets it down in front of me, I see a syringe full of lady. It's not mine, not the one I'd fixed up, but it's what I've been looking for all this time.

'But you should know that this won't take the edge off your hunger. We're giving it to you out of charity.'

I sit down in a corner of the room; I've never been shy about this stuff. I pick up the syringe and shoot up, my veins so tight that I can barely insert the needle. It's really hard to get it in, as if my skin were made of rubber or my veins had thinned out. When I finally manage to press the mix in there, I know it's the best heroin I've ever tried, although I don't even feel the kick. Just that I'm suddenly not hungry any more, and at the same time I'm sleepy. It feels like they've given me something I haven't received in a long time: permission to rest.

'Who are you talking to?' asks the teenager, alarmed, but I can't hear the girl's reply. Just like in the old days, my mind shakes off this world and starts ranging free. The heroin no longer has any effect on my senses; there's just hunger and anxiety. She's lit some incense that slowly fills the room with dense smoke, and in the smoke I see the shapes of my memories.

They're recent ones: memories of myself wandering El Zapotal. It's my lost time. I see crowds of people watching me from the bushes, from abandoned houses, whispering among themselves. I see people peering over the hacienda walls, their hazy silhouettes in the distance, aware that I'm here, I'm coming closer, I'll join them sooner or later. I see a body lying very still in a cot, as grey as the smoke his body coheres in, surrounded by presences murmuring worriedly. It's me, but I see it all from the outside, like in a dream, or like a spectre. I feel the edges of a narrow box descending past the earth's crust. It has a human shape, and it instantly evaporates into the smoke. All that's left is residue, particles lingering, floating shapeless, curling forth from the fragrant herbs like a stream of water, a plume of wind.

They're all memories from the other side, things you can't remember when you're alive. It's as if my eyes focus and can suddenly see that the dish I'd been given contained nothing but a splash of milk. The sense of touch returns to my body, and I feel like the ragged clothes I've been wearing are like a shadow, immaterial, dissolving on contact, and under them, the same thing happens to my skin, my flesh, even my floating, pulsing entrails, which go translucent, then transparent, and only the vague outline of my skeleton remains subtly stamped onto the fabric of the air.

I've been dead for some time, though I couldn't say how long. I've been wandering around town, tormenting the locals, sobbing, writing from the other side. Everything

I'd been doing while alive, I've kept doing it in death. I've even been shooting up something that could only have been ghost H, smoking cigarettes that could only have been ghost cigarettes.

'How long have I been dead?' I ask when I emerge from the fog.

'Here on earth, five months,' she says. 'Five months of your moaning and shrieking.'

'That's impossible. I can't have spent more than three weeks here.'

'It was almost half a year ago. They put you in the graveyard, but you couldn't keep still. Then they had to get you out of Don Tomás's place.'

'They kicked me out. They took all my things and threw me out onto the street to die.'

'But you were already dead,' she insists. 'They had to burn your syringe so no one else could use it. That's why you can't find it. We were there, we went with Tomás and Don Rutilo to bury you with your little tin box, your pencil and your notebook. Don Tomás even put some cigarettes in there. Not that it's kept you from moaning and complaining and being ungrateful. That's what's the matter with you. You were pacing around town before we'd even filled your grave.'

'Rutilo,' I say. 'That fucking cop has done nothing but kick me out of every spot I try to take shelter in. It's his fault I'm haunting the place.'

'Rutilo isn't a cop,' she corrects me. 'He's a witch doctor. Him and me, and the dogs and maybe a few little kids, and a few of the dead, we're the only ones who can see you at all. The others can only hear you whimpering in pain, banging on the windows, dragging your feet as you come and go. They can smell you and they feel a cold wind when you come close. The townspeople paid Rutilo to get you on your way, to help you rest. He was the one who turned up and pressured Otilia Sierra to pay what you were owed. That's the only way he could get you out of Don Tomás's place.'

Nothing makes sense any more.

'What about you?' I ask. 'Why can you see me?'

She gives me a long look and says nothing. But she shifts her head to show me how her neck and arms are stamped with burns like tree branches extending all over her body, and I realise that she's just like me, or what I used to be; she too has crossed the threshold into death.

'The trouble with living in such a small, sad town,' she says, 'is that sometimes the dead are better company than the living. That's why we hang out here, and in the graveyard, to see if we run into anyone we can talk with for a while.'

The brothers' eyes shift among the candle flame, their sister, and each other, while the teenager crouches outside the circle, head bowed between his legs. So these were the famous death-worshippers Rubí had told me about: a little gang of vagrant kids who hold spiritualist sessions in abandoned houses to keep from losing their minds with boredom.

'This kid can see you too,' the girl says, putting an arm around the crusty-eyed boy, who hasn't taken his eyes from me the whole time. The swelling hides his terror at first glance.

'But why?'

She hugs him and gives him a little shake, trying to encourage him to speak.

He lowers his head. In a weepy, faltering voice, he says 'The village kids dared me to rub the goo in a dog's eyes into mine. It made me see dead people. Now they say I'm crazy and they want to put me in a home. So I left and came here with the others.' He gestures to the group of kids.

'That's how his eyes got infected,' the girl says, wiping the muck from them and smoothing his hair.

I watch them for a few minutes, feeling only a sense of great injustice. So I've been reduced to a hungry spectre drifting around the village, begging for the only thing I believe can fill the hole inside me. Everyone seems to know it except for me. It's the birth of a new feeling in me, something I've never let myself feel before – a vague but penetrating sense of shame.

'Why didn't anyone tell me I was already dead?'

The girl's expression softens into a warm smile. 'That's just not how it's done, amigo. It's etiquette, plain and simple. Would you wake up a sleepwalker? No, you'd just try to get him back into bed. You'd try to convince him to get some rest…'

'Okay, stop it already,' the teenager interrupts, terrified. 'There's no one there. Who are you guys talking to?'

No one answers. I try to make sense of when I could have passed over to the other side. It's strange to migrate unwittingly into another world, but I've been on this journey for a long time; the route has become my daily routine. It's hard to pinpoint exactly when I made my crossing, because I shifted very quickly from being dead in life to being the living dead, and it's not like the transition had much of an impact on my experience. Both sides of the border are the same desolate plain, extending as far as the eye can see. I've spent most of my days famished and wretched, ignored by others, my body in a state of partial decomposition. In a sense, death has been my element, my natural state, for quite a while.

I go back over my arrival to this place, my feverish nights of opium hallucinations. It's like trying to figure out when exactly you fell asleep and began to dream. When did things become so different, so drained of colour? When was time shattered into chaos, rendered ragged, irregular, caught in an endless cycle? It's been going on for ages. I try to recall the last time I ate, or shat, and it was so long ago that I can't remember. I'm no longer hungry for food, not even for smack. I don't even know what this hunger is – the hunger that gnaws at us ghosts.

I struggle to pinpoint when I started seeing the dead, or when they started to see me; when I found myself all alone in this town, frozen in time. But I've been carrying the dead with me for years, and I've always been alone. Time has always been an experience of torture between one rush and the next. I try to organise my memories, my last night in a bar, the incident at Antonio Sierra's farm, my naked funeral march in the rain, until the fix of lady I shot up just before they took me out to the cemetery.

That fix I'd prepared with such devotion, with such love, the fix that had me roaming all over town for days. Of course I hadn't found it, of course I'm dead: that must have been the final shot, the one that finally sent me over to the other side.

'They say it's a peaceful feeling,' she says suddenly.

She's still watching me, kneeling to one side of the circle, her face glowing dimly in the candlelight. The teenager lowers his head, doesn't want any part of this. The twins keep avoiding my eyes. But now I know why: none of the three can see me.

'I didn't feel a thing,' I say, 'but it's been a long time since I felt anything at all. Even so, I'm sad I didn't get to experience that.'

'Didn't your loved ones come to guide you?'

I thought for a moment. It all seemed pretty pathetic in retrospect.

'I think my dog tried. But I ignored him.'

'What about the Virgin?' she asks. 'Didn't you see the Virgin? Didn't any spirits come to lead you into the light before you fell back down here?'

'I can't remember. I woke up in the graveyard. When I got kicked out of my room, I went looking for Juan. He told me to go to All-Souls' Hill, and that's where I was going when I saw you.'

'If you saw the guardian of the door,' she says, 'he offered you a way in. Why didn't you take it?'

'It was far and I was scared I wouldn't make it. I wanted to see if I could find a little lady for the road.'

She looks down and shakes her head. 'Then your soul really is sick.'

We all sit in silence around the candle, the fragrant smoke curling through the room. I feel like I've succumbed to a scam, like when I was sold a packet of cinnamon instead of horse, a little like all those people must have felt when I stopped them on the street and asked for money. I feel like I'd been caught off guard, that no one had properly explained the rules, that the ship had set sail without me. This time, what I missed in a moment of distraction and stupidity, of fear – it wasn't a bundle of bills or a packet of smack, it wasn't the kit with the sweetest fix I'd ever cooked, not the love of my life gone purple after hours of choking on her own vomit. It was my whole life, and with it any chance to participate in life on earth.

'What's in that dish?' I ask.

'An offering, to take the edge off your hunger.'

'I want some more. Just a little.'

'No, I can't do anything else for you now. If you run into the doorman again, I suggest you accept his invitation.'

With a mix of puzzlement and wonder, the teenager watches her speaking. And when we fall back into a heavy silence, he breaks it: 'What is he saying?'

He talks about me as if I weren't there, but he catches his breath when the girl replies. She weighs her words carefully, looking at me: 'Sometimes people are filled with desires they can never satisfy during their lives. Not even death can fix that. Their souls roam the world, trying to sate their hunger, but they can't. Their bellies are big as mountains, but their mouths are tiny and narrow as pins. They're condemned to being hungry forever. This one's veins shrunk on him, poor guy. He's trying to figure out where to go now, because here... well, he can't stay here any longer.'

The boy can't believe it. As a last resort against his fear, he starts to mock her. He says she's always been the crazy one, the weird girl in town, everyone knew it ever since she hugged the transformer when her brothers died in that sawmill accident. No one was surprised she kept setting a place at the table for her brothers after all that. Now, to keep his grip on his own sanity, the boy thinks the crazy chick just wants to scare them.

The twins don't so much as open their mouths as they sit there. They're the dead brothers, as it turns out, and they're wandering around in death, following their sister, watching the candles, glancing at each other and themselves, keeping very quiet. I hadn't understood until then that they too belong to the secret club Mike had always talked about. I ask the girl why, if they're dead, I can see them but they can't see me.

'The dead see only what they damn well please,' she says.

Which is something the living do as well.

16

Who would have thought? Death isn't like I imagined. Lots of people had warned me I could wake up dead any day now and not even realise. I'd come to El Zapotal to take that decision wholeheartedly, to put an end to it all, and to make sure I wouldn't miss it – to make sure I really felt the rush that would be followed by nothing but peace. Now that I can see things as they truly are, I know it was all a trap: the trap the lady set for me so I'd stay with her. What I felt, that flash of peace – that wasn't death. It couldn't be, because I'd always come back. And there's no coming back from death. I'm never coming back from this one, I'm sure of it.

If I'd known that passing over onto the other side would just be more of the same, the idea would have been unbearable to me and I never would have left the city in the first place. It's a shame there's no such thing as heroin for the soul, and my body – the only thing that understands the lady – is now six feet underground. At this point it won't be easy to get it back. What tears at me from the inside, though, is knowing that I missed the big show, and now I'm starting to wonder what else I missed while I was alive – missed because I was burning time away, passed out on a rush with my lady.

It makes all the sense in the world that I'm still roaming around here, that I'd felt the strength returning to my limbs: this body I feel isn't the body I was given at birth. I'm creating it myself, little by little, with whatever remnants of consciousness I've got left. I'm making it out of what I can remember about inhabiting a body. The bittersweet sensation of my stomach ulcer, the stabbing ache of my bones against my flesh, the searing heat and constant itch crawling over every centimetre of my skin. It gives me a comforting illusion of solidity, helps me reconnect with what things were like. Everything I've done until now has been a futile attempt to reconstruct what it meant to be alive. That's why I've been searching so desperately for the lady. I never understood what was happening during my life. It's no surprise that death is the same.

I had to leave the cabin. The smoke was starting to suffocate me; I think that's why they lit the incense. They wished me a good journey as I left. A good journey where, I thought. There's still a trace of will in me, and that's the only reason why I'm still here. I must have that one last bit of business to attend to. All I can see in the dark are the windows of a few houses that seem to glow from the inside. I get closer, peer in. These openings I've been peeking into for days are the mirrors of the houses, and I'm moving through them. They're one of my only windows onto the world of the living.

The others are candles. Sometimes it's like I'm travelling across a vast empty space, shapeless, bereft of any presences, no stars in the sky, and I'm guided only by tiny flickers of light in the darkness, which I grope my way towards until they grow large enough for me to see that they're actually lit candles. They've become my only points of reference, and I move from one candle to another among the living. Sometimes I come across people sleeping, sometimes guys drinking, or a family eating beans for dinner. I hear them talk about hunger and heartbreak. Troubles of the living. None ever turns to look my way.

The church and graveyard are filled with candles, shining from within, but there's a chaotic noise that keeps me from drawing any closer. They must be teeming with the dead. I don't even know what I'm looking for any more, but I know I'll keep roaming, hungry, searching. I don't want to live a ghost's life, smoking and eating and raiding shrines until the end of my days, or when the relevant authorities decide I'm ready for absolution. I know I can't haunt the town, threatening people so that they'll set out bowls of milk on their doorsteps if they want to spend a peaceful, silent night, a night without the shouts and howls of the afflicted. I don't want to be subjected to exorcisms over and over until they trap me in a jar or something. I want to get out of here. I want to rest.

It distresses me to wonder how long I'll have to keep meandering this way. But maybe it has something to do with my goal at the very start: to find some sort of meaning in this experience, even if it's just for me and no one else. Maybe that's the point of this notebook. Maybe this account I'm drawing up before I cross the threshold isn't something that has happened to me alone; maybe it's what the Tibetans call the bardo. If so, it's nothing like I imagined. I thought it would be more... I don't know. More spectacular, I guess.

Valerie got into *The Tibetan Book of the Dead* and gave me a copy once. Just read it, she told me, even just once, even if you don't understand a thing. I did read it and I didn't understand a thing. According to the book, it's what you see when you die: the bardo. That's what they call it. They say you see your life parade before your eyes, and you have visions of monsters with a bajillion arms and skull necklaces and blades, then lights and people fucking. The book says you shouldn't be scared when the monsters turn up because they're not real, they're just there to freak you out and distract you, because you're supposed to stay alert for some brightly coloured lights that appear right after the monsters and just before the people fucking, and those are like express lanes to the other side.

They say a white light shines first, and if you catch that one, you're all set. You become cosmically enlightened and live forever in the radiant gleam of the absolute. Clearly I missed that boat. But if you don't catch it, other lights appear, and you can nab those and be reborn. I don't know if I want to be reborn – I've always thought it would be a total drag to start all over, especially since I know that birth is like being Naloxone-zapped out of an OD and straight into withdrawal. Under the circumstances, though, I think being reborn would still be better than the alternative, which is just to keep wandering here. Anyway, that book describes everything as really spectacular. Nothing like what's been happening to me. Who would have thought – those Tibetans in their flowy robes were all just full of shit.

I don't have anywhere to go any more, I'm an aimless soul, a migrant who knows that things on the other side are exactly the same, or worse. Before, at least there was the steady heat of flesh pumping blood, faint and feverish, and there were wishes to chase and opium dreams. At least that kept you going. You were still living in the tangible, manipulable world of neurochemistry. Now there's no chemistry to alter, no stomach to fill. I no longer know what I'm supposed to look for, or long for, make sense of, resolve. Those are pleasures reserved for the living.

Before, too, at least there were sensations that came from the outside, like air caressing your skin; there was sunlight seeping into you and your surroundings, and colours. Not this, not fragments of entrapped light, mere echoes ricocheting haphazardly around a dark chamber, not these residual impressions. Before, at least there were people around, not this total solitude and desolation. You could go to a bar, have them crowd around you and harangue you to put a bullet in your head, and you could refuse. In death, we're really alone. Like in life, only more. Or at least that's true for me.

I've been travelling this road for quite some time now. I spent my whole life chasing people away; it's only fitting that I'd become a monster, or a ghost. Who knows where my mum went, where Mike and Valerie and all my friends went, but they're certainly not here. At long last, I pulled it off: I'm completely alone. Now I really do have time to think about my life. I think that's the true hell, especially if you spent it like I did. If only you could find a way to live that would make life after death more comforting, more enjoyable. I don't even remember my happiest moments, and what I do remember haunts me, keeps me up at night. There's something about life that doesn't let you ever be alone, but in death you have no choice.

The only thing that accompanies me is the jungle. It's still lush with flowers, and on the side of the path I find fruit that looks like pink apples. Sometimes I pick one up, give it a sniff, and take a bite, captive to a strange curiosity; its dry, porous flesh squeaks between my teeth and smells like bitter dirt. Everything has smelled and tasted like dirt for days, as if my nose and mouth were coated with it. I know I won't sate my hunger by eating this fruit, but even so, gnawing and swallowing it sets off something inside me. It's as if my whole being were a tangle of electrical currents held together by memory, a jumble of recollections that spark and crackle as I tug at them. Being alive makes for a close relationship with matter. All that's left of me is oblivion, and once even my forgetfulness has dissipated, maybe then I can finally rest.

The jungle watches me, dark and looming in every direction, like a living wall, a guardian entity tasked with keeping me confined to its domain. Water courses through; I can hear the trickling rivulets. Sometimes I consider kneeling on the bank to drink, but I know I could gulp down all the water on the hillside and it wouldn't be enough to quench my thirst. I lose myself in the labyrinth of ridges, clearings, twists and turns, and I wander, as I watched so many others wandering before me. I hope I don't run into anyone – that would probably be as frightening for me as for them.

Not long ago I came across a shepherd who had fallen asleep in a glade. A dusky light still shone in the air, and I approached him through the fog, drawing close enough to see the cadence of his breath as his belly rose and fell. I've never been ambitious enough to feel envy, but I think I did feel something like it towards that man. There's something enviable about the transient state of living, in the pleasure of being able to satiate your hunger with food, drown your sorrows with tears or drink, then succumbing to physical fatigue after hours of labour. Surrendering the body to sleep. Even the act of breathing – a reliable way to alleviate the body's sense of asphyxiation in its natural state – is enviable to me.

I must have got too close, because he jolted awake. He even fixed his eyes on me, but then he quickly looked away, calmed down and went back to sleep. When he wakes again, he won't even remember he saw me. There was a time I would have thought he was ignoring me for being a disgusting junkie, trying to drive me away. Now I know that the living ignore the dead to be left in peace. That's all. They don't do it on purpose; it's a habit they've acquired so they can carry on without endless sermons or complaints from them. The shepherd can't see me. Only the dogs can see me now. I don't know if they followed me out of town or caught my trail after the fact. They helped me down the slope and led me back into the village.

'Hey Bonesy,' they say, smiling their doggy smiles, 'where to now?'

And I reply, 'Someplace where I can get some sleep.'

They convinced me to return to the graveyard. I've been lying under my tree for a long time. The tree they buried me under, rather; there are so many of us here that I can't call it mine. I've kept very still, waiting to see if it does any good, but one thing is certain: I can't sleep any more. Sleep is for the body, not the soul, and buried here, six feet below me, I'm sure that my body is resting. For me, though, death is a long spell of insomnia in which I occasionally lose consciousness, and when I come to I know I've been roaming aimlessly for all this time, without any rhyme or reason, without knowing exactly what it is I'm looking for now.

I'm not sure how long I've lingered in this spot where day never truly dawns. I don't like the graveyard because of the noise: when the sky clears a little, the living come to mourn, and at night, which is almost all the time, it's like a dance hall out here. The dead come out to socialise, or else to complain. It's like they enjoy being stuck in this place, not to mention going out and scaring kids, unsettling mules, bewitching people and houses. They're like good old Chachi: they've settled down in limbo, halfway to the land they wanted to get to in the first place.

When the other dead come too close, I growl at them, tell them to leave me alone, let me write, that in any case I'm not even from here, I'm just passing through. The same things I always said. From their reactions, it's clear that they see me as the newbie in jail. They laugh because I think I'm heading for an early release and can't imagine what's in store. They say that this is a sad, lonely place, so why don't I come chat. When I was still alive and wanted to rest, no one would leave me in peace then, either; it was all gossip, pressure, favours. Resigning myself to the existence of the dead feels like a failure. That's what I did during my life, and there's something about the method that never really worked. I can see it now.

Lying here, I've had loads of time to think. I no longer feel the urge to chase my lady, or maybe I still do, but I know there's no point. Who would have thought that rehab would be so easy: all I had to do was kick the bucket. But even rehabilitation is nothing like I thought it would be. I'd already heard that when you leave the lady, you rediscover all the little pleasures you'd forgotten, the very stuff of life. Now I'm condemned to remembering those pleasures from where I lie: sleeping, eating, fucking. It's ridiculous, this whole business of coming round to life, understanding it only once you're already dead. People say it happens to the others too, that you can only understand life when you're too old to live it. So they say. But I don't know – and I'll never know, because I didn't make it to old age, and I never understood anything about life, either.

Now my carrion is perpetuating the balance of things. Maybe that's why I feel my skin crawling with ants, why I've had worms in my guts for days. The thought gives me a curious sense of pride: now I can finally say that I achieved my goal, I shed the shackles of the flesh and earthly affairs. Now I can say that I'm made entirely of spirit, and the things of this world can't hold me back, they're no longer any business of mine. But I'd have to admit that I miss them constantly.

I'd have to admit that this isn't the end I expected, ringed by a radiant halo of light. It's not something I'd be proud to flaunt in front of the people I left behind. If I could see them, maybe I'd try to offer a warning. I bet many of them tried to warn me back then, like good old Mike. You don't listen, you think your brain's all eaten away by drugs, you're hallucinating, and that's all true, but you'd do well to heed the warnings just the same. It's like they're telling you, 'Don't come over here, man, it really sucks in here, stay out there and enjoy your life, since you're lucky enough to still be living it.' But you do it anyway. You never learn from warnings. You always figure it out the hard way.

If I'd thought of all this before, maybe I would have done things differently, although who knows, maybe I would've done them exactly the same. I don't like being called a coward, because you need real balls to do what I did. But who am I fooling? I'm terrified. The idea of existing like this is terrifying. I don't know if what scares me most is the thought of eternity, or that everything could stay just like this, static, never changing, remaining exactly as it was when I was alive. That sounds worse than any hell I've ever heard about. Matter has the benefit of transience, occurring in a state of constant flux and trans-formation. Pleasures don't last long, but pain passes too. Here, in the plane I find myself in now, is where the life sentence was invented. Even if I make it out someday, every second here feels like forever.

17

I went to El Rincón de Juan to see if it was finally open, but the padlock was still barring the entrance, and no matter how hard I look, no matter how long I wait, the guardian of the door is nowhere to be found. So I drift around town, as I did in the past, and observe the living, and once I overstay my welcome, the dogs lead me back to the graveyard.

A little while ago I saw a woman bathing in the river. I stayed for a bit to watch – not even with lust, but as you'd listen to a sad song that evokes some beautiful faraway time you didn't fully enjoy in the moment and have now lost forever. And the song will be over soon, too. She'd gone to meet a man in the woods, where no one could see them making love. It was a furious kind of love, as if they were putting their whole lives into it, because they were. In the loneliness and desolation of the town, they were maybe the only two beings who could love each other that way. And they were trying to die in the attempt. The living work alchemy with their desire, almost always by accident, and it's a moving and unsettling spectacle. They make lives like ours, like mine, which start and end without us really understanding what happened to us. And it was this. This is what happened to us.

I knew I was witnessing a conception: the product of an accident caused by the passion between two beings. This scene will remain a mystery to that new creature, a prehistoric moment that will always exist beyond the reaches of their memory. I watched them bite and scratch as if they wanted to tear off each other's skin, devour each other, kill each other – and yet they were giving life. From the outside, there seemed to be no difference: the intensity of the act was the very same. I watched them and felt the yearning in my guts, the yearning for being alive.

I wonder if the living know we watch them. I wonder if they imagine that most of what we do, us dead people, is done without any passion at all, but out of routine, habit, boredom, just because there's time to spare. I don't think so, I doubt they get it; I never gave it any thought. It's disturbing to make contact with us, and it upsets the living, they'd rather not know we exist at all. Which is why we can watch without interference, and they don't change their behaviour just because we're there.

The material existence of the living is a comedy of monumental errors, and first-class entertainment for the dead. Maybe that's its real purpose. You end up realising that you didn't do so bad at the end of the day. There are people who sacrifice everything they love, and struggle their entire lives for things far less satisfying than a shot of lady. There are people who let their lives slip away without ever setting foot outside, never going on a quest as important as getting Valerie her fix was to me. Some never lose friends like the ones I lost, like Mike and Jairo, like Elisa and Romuel, and Úrsula and Valerie, and so many others, because they never had them to begin with, because they don't know what it's like to be in the trenches with your friends, staving off hunger together, watching them drop like flies in the sun, taking care of each other when the shakes hit, making bone marrow soup for breakfast to make it through, to keep from drying up inside. They don't know what it's like. They live their sad little lives all alone, sadder and littler and lonelier than me. Now I have to stay put and do penance for all of them, but I understand, I accept it. It's not so bad in the end, because I can make at least a bit of sense out of it all, even if it's just a very little bit, even if it's only for me.

I'd like to tell my friends the whole story, but I can't shake the feeling that I'm the drop-out, the flunkie, the dumbest kid in class. Eventually you grasp that life is actually a lot like a rehab clinic, and if you last longer than your buddies it only means that you're the most fucked-up of them all, the one who most needed the lesson. If I ever saw them again, or my Valerie, I'd inevitably feel ashamed. What a relief that heaven is a myth, that there's nowhere to reunite with your dead. I think that place would feel like hell. Maybe it does exist, but not for me. I'd rather rove around here and never have to face anyone.

I think there was a time when I did hope to see Valerie again, but maybe it's better this way. It would be kind of ridiculous to apologise at this point. I think she'd laugh at me. I'd have to admit that we missed our chance because I got distracted, and not just for a moment, but for entire years. I'd have to admit, only now that it's too late and our bodies are too crumbled for love, that I'm starting to feel lucid. And I remember the very last date with my lady.

Valerie was an empty shell by then, and her eyes couldn't focus on anything. The last time I saw her brighten was the day she pulled me close, whispered into my ear, and asked if we could go on one final date. Cook up a fix and never get up again. We'd been hooked for so long that all I wanted was to see her let go. I said yes, I thought it was a great idea, her wish was my command.

I think that's why I forget things. Because if I remembered them, I'd have to acknowledge I knew perfectly well that the fix I cooked would only get me as far as the entrance. I'd have to admit that I knew this stuff: I understood that while Val choked and sputtered, I'd be floating far away, and I wouldn't even notice when she'd finally taken the step. That's why I don't like being called a coward. There are plenty of things I don't regret, but I do regret that. We would have been able to lead each other by the hand. And maybe then I could have avoided what happened after.

I don't know what I was clinging to so hard. I never had anything, only desire. I always thought I wasn't a clinger, that my desire was the first thing to die. But it turns out to be the strongest thing of all, and all that's left of me. Now that even this has stirred in the underworld of my consciousness, maybe I'll fade away until I vanish. But I doubt it. There's something in all of us that never disappears. Now I understand why my Val wanted me to read *The Tibetan Book of the Dead*. The masks fall away, and the monsters are no longer menacing in the shadows. I wonder what happens now, if the effervescence of desire starts to dissipate all by itself, or if there's a way back to what used to be earthly time. I wish I had a body to make love with, to do something with this desire I carry with me everywhere I go.

At least I've got the living to make me laugh once in a while. The dead are all about hunger and sorrows. There aren't many, really, who lived to be dead, but the living are exuberant, always running around and getting themselves all worked up, moaning and flailing about.

It's sweet, how innocently and seriously they take things. It makes you want to tell them, 'Hey, kiddo, why so anxious? Relax, have a shot of lady and you'll see that none of it matters.' Really, though, who do you think you are, dispensing advice? It's not like things worked out so great for you. Better to keep your mouth shut, since it's all silence in the end, and you're already lucky enough to have disentangled yourself from everything. Or almost everything.

18

Sometimes I still feel like I have a part to play in all this. I feel like it's not just for me, that I'm part of something bigger, that maybe I showed up and stayed because there were people who needed to find me. A few have seen me already. I don't know exactly what it is they see, but judging by their reactions, I must be even more terrifying than I was in life. People scream Bible verses at you and run off. Or they toss salt at you. Others even try to exorcise you and shit like that, and you're even open to it. If it works, why not? But it never does. Rutilo appears and puts on his whole show, chanting and incense and the whole nine yards, and they flood you with smoke and exhort you and so on and so forth, but it doesn't do fuck-all.

'I already told you that I would've left ages ago if I could. I'm stuck here with you, just like you're stuck here with me.'

Some never recover. I don't know why some can see me and others can't. I don't think I have any say in the matter. Who knows why some folks were destined for a fright and others aren't, why some people are doomed to chance upon a hungry, skeletal spectre with floating guts and skin turned inside-out while walking in the woods or through town in the middle of the night; why they have to bump right into a reeking, horrifying creature that instantly shrinks back with shyness, wariness, and shame, and tries to avoid them despite their morbid curiosity. They must know I'm dead. No one ever took an interest in me when I was alive, never sought me out like this. Sometimes I think the whole thing must be more about them than about me. Maybe the world is like a mirror, and they end up seeing me because they're hungry too, drifting through their lives, whimpering with fear and pain. Maybe I'm some kind of warning.

I've been thinking about it for a while, because I do feel like I have something in common with every one of the dead people I saw, or most of the ones I can remember. I'm just like the little girl who trudges around, crying over her lost dog, or like Antonio Sierra, trying to make amends with his wife after death. I'm just like the drunk who asked me to spare some change for a drink. I'm thirsty, too. I'm not saying that none of them ever existed, because they do exist, or existed, just like me. I existed. I don't think I hallucinated them, even if reality is indistinguishable from my opium dreams, and those ghosts must be a figment of the schizophrenia that overcomes us addicts when our brain chemistry goes to shit. Even so, I don't think I hallucinated them, just as I don't think I'm anyone else's hallucination. Although I guess I am, in a sense. It's the only way I can exist now: as a spectral vision roaming everywhere and nowhere, visible to some and not to others.

It's getting harder to differentiate between reality and my own ravings, but that's been the case for so long that I've come to wonder if there's any difference at all. Maybe they're one and the same, part of a single experience that transcends both life and death, dreams and waking. Which must mean that those flowy-robed Tibetans weren't full of shit after all. Here in the bardo, you do run into all kinds of beings that let you pass – or not – through the underworld and towards the light, and the only way to cross the threshold is to know that none of it is real. They're projections on a curtain, tests that distract you and keep you lost in the labyrinth of your own mind, your habits, the desires you fed until they got so strong that they survived your earthly life, survived you.

This town, El Zapotal, is just a reflection of the isolation and emptiness inside me. That's why I ended up here. Maybe I never left the city at all, maybe I died back there in my cot and the whole journey through this godforsaken village has been the bardo, a voyage through the twenty-fourth circle of hell. What do I know. Life and death are a single continuum, two sides of the same coin. In my current state, I myself don't know if I'm real or a trail of memories snagged in the ether. I can't say whether the whole world is just a light show, an illusion. I didn't know if ghosts were real when I was alive, or if spirits and demons stalked the world. I had no proof, no certainties. Now I'm not sure if the living exist, either.

Sometimes I feel like I start to drift out as I write, just like I did on H. I feel the sky clearing, and the heat of a star on the memory of my skin lulls me almost into sleep. But when I look up, all I find is the same grey, starless, overcast expanse that's been suspended above me for days. I feel myself falling into something like a stupor, and I only snap out of it when I hear the dogs coming to find me, scratching at my grave, trying to get me up. So I come out and take a walk into town, leave the comforting terrain of the graveyard and embark in search of that light, that warmth, ready to seek and yearn, as I always have.

I'm looking for traces of whatever's warm and sweet. Death doesn't ask us to move on, but urges us back, back towards the origin of everything. I make the rounds through my usual spots, past the tree my body will be buried under forever, down the streets of El Zapotal and around El Rincón de Juan, until my steps lead me back to the room at Don Tomás's place and to that corner, the warmest I ever found in this place, and start fumbling around for the loose brick in the concrete wall, the one Mike once pulled out before he slipped away through a crack.

I've been rattling around for a while now, in the room where I spent my first days in town, and which is now fully built, painted and furnished, although I've never seen the tenants who live here now. I'm certain that they do hear me, though, scraping between the bricks. Finally I manage to pry it loose and take a peek into what awaits me beyond.

On the other side is a dense darkness, like a threshold onto nothing. It's the place that exists beyond the walls, beyond every closed door, beyond the pipes leading nowhere: an absence of place. That's where I'm going; there's nowhere to hide. The only feeling that stops me is something like a choked scream. It's fear, the deep terror I never let myself experience, only evaded in my torpor, my oblivion. The dogs smell that fear and urge me on. It horrifies me: any place, even one as dark and desolate as El Zapotal, is better than having no place at all.

'So what are you scared of, Bonesy, if the worst is already behind you?' they say. 'It's not like you can kick the bucket all over again, right?'

The dogs have a point. There's nothing left to fear. There's no life left, and the worst is over: I'm here now, and I'm not going anywhere. The fear crumbles with my decomposing body. I'm not that body any more, I'm not those aches and pains; it's all part of the panorama already. The loneliness and boredom aren't mine, but El Zapotal's. Poor, cursed, miserable town. I'm so grateful for everything it's done for me. Even that is dissipating now.

I know I'm bound to disappear, that even my ethereal trail will vanish from this place, and people won't ask too many times what happened to that Bonesy who was always hovering around town before they forget me for good. I wonder what happens once they do, and if it's possible to delve so deep into the darkness that everything disappears, even myself and this hint of consciousness still clinging insistently to the world. I'd never thought so much about my friends before. Maybe I too will reach the place where everyone's going, everything lost and forgotten.

I thought it would be easier to enter the void. But I've been sitting here in the corner for a long while, gathering my courage. I'm cold; I hope the feeling passes soon. I know there's no turning back, no lady, no warmth to be found, not for me. When I stare into the chink between the bricks, I see something that looks like blood mixing down in there, dark enough to resemble the dense matter that fills the universe. I see motion in that darkness, like some demonic dance in the beyond. It's like a spiral alluring me, and I'm so captivated by it that when I glance over my shoulder I'm already deep inside the labyrinth, and Don Tomás's room is far away. I've already left it behind.

Inside the darkness is a path, like a tunnel, and as I move farther into it, I feel like I'm recovering my vision. My senses are stirring, my mind casting off its shackles, setting out to explore. I advance along the path, losing and regaining consciousness. The dogs follow, call me back when I lose the thread, keep me focused. I grope my way through the shadows beyond the walls, as if I could only find my way home by going backwards, into myself, instead of trying to leave the town. I find a staircase carved into the stone that spirals into the subsoil, and I descend the cold steps one by one. There's a dusty smell that reminds me of something very old, like childhood. I try to figure out what I'm seeing in the darkness, that dynamic pattern, like static on a screen, and then I know. It's a flock of birds, an enormous entity undulating in the wind.

Below are cool caves, someplace hidden in the depths, much vaster than the surface, and I think I remember that its cracks and crannies are inhabited by strange life forms taking cover from what's above. This is the deepest, most secret place, and I know I'll only see it once; anyone who returns to it will no longer be me. Here are the foundations, the lowest possible bedrock I can ever reach on this voyage. Nothing disappears, even if it's forgotten, not even myself. Everything ends here, underground.

I feel like I've already walked around these parts, maybe in an opium dream. I feel enveloped in an earthly blanket that welcomes and protects me from the elements lurking outside. This is the origin of all things, the road home, a cavernous, uterine universe that gathers me close as it did once before. It's as if I were retracing my steps to rediscover a familiar place, and I start to feel a rush of emotion, like wings beating in my belly.

The tingling I feel is a lot like being a child, or being in love. It's so intense that there are moments when I wish it would stop, but when I wonder what might replace it, I know there's nothing before or after. This is all there is. All I can do is keep going, moving forward, giving, giving. You try to give of yourself before you realise you're nothing. Being nothing, all I want is to become something, and in this way maybe I live; maybe

I am, just a little. I continue my procession through the remnants of memory, through a shapeless dark, which seems to cool and sharpen around me for the first time in ages.

It's not light I see at the end of the cave, but another kind of darkness, denser, more intimate. The dogs have been trailing me through the tunnels, and they're still here when we reach the mouth of the cavern. Now that I can see them more clearly, it seems that their faces are growing more and more human. I don't know when they started to look like that, or if they always did, like werewolves, chatty lycanthropes guiding me under the canopy, towards a thicket so overgrown that it looks impenetrable. We're so deep inside the jungle that if I lose track of the dogs I won't ever find my way out.

Since I don't know where I'm going, I have no choice but to follow them into the shadowy under-brush. The fatigue in my bones no longer slows me down, and I move closer to that familiar place, warm and comforting. I'm coming home. The exuberance I feel in my guts, in my limbs, in my fingers, this sensation I know so well, is like the sickness abating, like the lady coming to visit.

I can't say where the feeling comes from, because I never had a home like this when I was alive. But when I see the cracked pink walls of the haciendas rising up before us like relics of another time, I know it's the only place for me. That's where I'm from, that's where I'm going. That's where I want to stay forever. I can hear a murmur from inside, a great assembly, a carnival, and as we reach the monumental corroded wood doors, the dogs are no longer dogs, but people, two boys from town.

'You know the drill, Bonesy,' one of them says. 'Don't get lost on us, that's the important part. Can you pay your way in?'

Confidently, I present them with the silver and emerald charms. But they just scoff and stuff the jewels into their pockets.

'These are worthless here. If you want in, you have to give up what you love most in the whole world.'

This is the tragedy of dying without a burial: no one looks out for you, for the path awaiting you after. You don't think about these things until it's too late. They could have buried me with my pet, or my most valued slave, or even just with my leather jacket, some toy I prized as a kid. Or maybe with the photo of my beloved, or a couple of silver coins. Even a pathetic little flower would have helped me now. But I hadn't received even that. I'd smoked the cigarettes I was given. I pat my pockets and all I find is the aluminium box with the kit inside: the opium pipe, a blackened old spoon, a dirty syringe, and that's that. I hold it out to the kids. One of them takes it, turns it over curiously, and gives it a shake; he hears the metallic rattle inside the tin. He opens it and studies its contents, then shows it to his friend.

Together, they take a moment to assess its value. Then one of them says, 'You're good. This'll work.'

I always knew I'd carry that tin all the way to the doors of the underworld. The gate swings open, and I feel the cold sweat, the prickling in my legs, my arms, my neck, the imminent rush. They stop me: before I go in, they say, I have to hand over everything, everything I've got. So I ask them to let me sit for a minute and take care of one last bit of business.

There I sit, at the doors of the hacienda, to finish telling what happened to me in all this time I've been wandering through limbo. I think I'm done now, I think I made at least a little sense of it, found some meaning in it all. I think I managed to do something constructive. If I'm ever reborn, I'll do things differently, I think, although who knows, maybe I'll do them exactly the same. Maybe, after we're born, we're bound to do the same as we do when we die: to roam the world, yearning, puzzling stuff out, trying to find happiness with our lady. I hope not; I hope life still has some surprises in store, just as death did. I don't know – I find it harder and harder to remember what it was like to be alive. Maybe I'll soon forget it altogether. In any case, I don't want to be reborn. This is the end of the road for me. Inside, a warm light glows, calling to me.

I still don't know what's awaiting me on the other side. Maybe I'll find the great trap house, the place where everyone who's got lost will gather, or I'll wake to the sound of my own weeping, coated in blood and vomit, surrounded by doctors and panicking people who slap my face and force me to breathe. This withdrawal I feel, this nostalgia for the womb, like a sickness, must be what people mean when they talk about 'life'. Now they're giving me over to the light. I'm going to surrender the kit, my notebook, and my pencil too, and then I'll go home. I'm going to meet my mother again. I can hear a tumult from inside, footfalls, movement, shouts and whispers calling for me, a *tum-ta-tum-ta-tum* like the drums of a wild celebration. They remember my name in there. I'm going to find the faces of my friends in the crowd and reunite at last with my señora.

I have a date with the lady, and I wouldn't miss it for the world.

TRANSLATOR'S NOTE

Soon after the Spanish publication of *Una cita con la Lady*, by Mateo García Elizondo, I joined him and several other writers for a launch event at the Guadalajara Book Fair. I'd only translated a sample of the book by then; we didn't yet know where or when it would end up published in English. It was the first time I'd ever heard Mateo speak publicly about his novel.

Four years later – and now that *Una cita con la lady* has taken on new lives in other languages, including this English version as *Last Date in El Zapotal* – I think often about something he said that night. Paraphrasing, of course, in the way that the passing of time and my own relationship with the book has invariably led me to do: *Last Date in El Zapotal* may seem like a book about death, but it's really a book about living. And about (here I am, editorialising flagrantly now) how difficult it is to stop.

This is a novel of in-betweenness: between life and death, the present and the past, solitude and communion, nihilism and desire. Its dogged liminality (with nods to Rulfo as much as to Kerouac) is borne out not just on the level of plot (a ravaged young junkie from the big city retreats to a rural village in hopes of ending his life with a fatal dose), but also in the materiality of García Elizondo's language. This is the terrain I wandered while translating *Last Date in El Zapotal*, the topographical map I traced with my fingertips.

The author's sentences drift and dilate, ripple outward with the tug of memory, snag on the edges of intervening thoughts. They can be as graceful as they are disconcerting, and they're often rooted in deliberate ambiguity: is this moment a now-moment or a then-moment? Where is the 'here' occupied by the main character at any given point? Who and what among the presences and landscapes he engages with are 'real'? Beyond the uncanniest, ghostliest moments of the story, shifting as it does between the land of the dead and the living world (rotten as this world too may be), I'm also interested in its depiction of memory itself as a kind of death-in-life, or vice-versa.

When I remember my first contact with the novel, this is what I remember drawing me in: the narrator's reveries, stupefied into nostalgia for his great lost love, his friendships, the companionship of his dog; his grim, sordid, hostile environment suddenly refracting and expanding to make room for tenderness, wistfulness, regret. Here, as in this passage about the start of an opium trip, García Elizondo's sentences ribbon outward, fluttering, folding back on themselves:

> ...I always feel like I can see a presence, sometimes more human, sometimes almost animal, as if the sky itself were a parted veil, offering a glimpse of a face that peers out and watches me, looks after me. It greets me for a moment, then vanishes again. It's a familiar presence, but I struggle to recognise it, and just as it starts to make sense to me, the cloud of birds

contracts again. The presence hides itself away and won't come back if I wait. It only returns when I forget, letting it catch me by surprise once more...

But before long, he always finds himself deposited abruptly back in the dark: in his hovel of a rented room, in a dingy bar, in the shadowy brush on the outskirts of town, in one nightmare or another.

As a translator, my preoccupation was to keep my finger on this erratic pulse, not just defending but also feeding its ebb and flow. 'Dreamlike' is a word we might use to describe something ethereal and alluring just as readily as something sinister, macabre. I wanted my English prose to keep its hands plunged into both of these textures (oneiric curiosity, nightmarish dread), mixing them together as deliberately as the author did.

I'm fond of a prose poem called 'Meditations in an Emergency', by Cameron Awkward-Rich. 'There's a dream I have in which I love the world,' it reads. Of all the possible dreams to be found in *Last Date in El Zapotal* – fever dreams, opium dreams, phantasmagorical limbo-dreams, heroin hazes, memories as bleak as nightmares – this is the dream that rises to the surface of the novel for me. The dream of love, the dream for love, the dream of what it would mean for love to be enough, to have been enough before it was lost. Translating Mateo García Elizondo was, for me, a way to explore the materialisation of such dreams, their gauzy grammar flickering in the dark.

Robin Myers
Buenos Aires, September 2023

CHARCO PRESS

Director & Editor: Carolina Orloff
Director: Samuel McDowell

www.charcopress.com

Last Date in El Zapotal was published on
80gsm Munken Premium Cream paper.

The text was designed using Bembo 11.5 and ITC Galliard.

Printed in March 2024 by TJ Books Limited
Padstow, Cornwall, PL28 8RW using responsibly
sourced paper and environmentally-friendly adhesive.